Wolf Point

Wolf Point

EDWARD FALCO

UNBRIDLED

BOOKS

Unbridled Books
Denver, Colorado

Originally published as an Unbridled Books hardcover
First paperback edition, 2006.

Library of Congress Cataloging-in-Publication Data

Falco, Edward.
Wolf Point / Edward Falco.
p. cm.
Hardcover edition ISBN 1-932961-08-9
Paperback edition ISBN 10: 1-932961-30-5
ISBN 13: 978-1-932961-30-0
1. Middle aged men—Fiction.   2. Life change events—Fiction.
3. Hitchhiking—Fiction.   I. Title.
PS3556.A367W65 2005
813'.54—dc22
2005015902

1   3   5   7   9   10   8   6   4   2

Book Design by SH • CV

First Printing

Wolf Point

At age fifty-seven, dressed in faded blue jeans and a black cashmere sweater, with silver-gray hair and a lean, muscular build, T slowed down in his new Land Rover on Route 81 approaching Syracuse, New York. On the side of the road a pulp tableau coalesced: a young woman somewhere between eighteen and twenty-one in red leather pants over black boots and a white silk blouse opened three buttons down, with blond hair flying out from her head wild and wind blown and radiant in the horizontal light of late afternoon, put one foot up on a black guitar case and stuck out her arm in hitchhiker pose. Behind her, completing the warning image, the only-a-fool-would-stop vignette, an older, long-haired, black-leather-jacket-clad boy leaned back into the roadside foliage as if hoping he wouldn't be noticed. T knew better than to stop, which was why he did, veering to the shoulder and rolling past them as the girl trotted toward him, leaving the guy to pick up the guitar case and follow.

"This is funny," he whispered to himself, encased in the as yet undisturbed atmosphere of his SUV. He twisted around in the driver's seat just as the girl hesitated at the rear door. She bent down slightly to look into the front of the Rover, to check him out. Their eyes met and for an instant they held each other's gaze. She might be twenty-one but more likely eighteen or nineteen. He'd have bet his Porsche, from that one look, that she had summed him up as one more concupiscent old guy, easily manipulated.

He pushed a button and all the Rover's locks popped up. The girl flung open the rear door and then cheerfully got in the front and started undoing a series of laces on her boots. "My feet are killing me," she said, the vowels of each word slightly elongated. Her boots rose up to midcalf so that she had to peel back the leather pants to undo the complicated crisscross of laces, folding herself over in a position that left him free to gaze unobserved at her mostly exposed breasts, a fact of which he understood she was totally aware. "I am so grateful you stopped," she said, and abandoned her work for a moment to look his way with a radiant smile and touch his thigh lightly as a brief gesture of thanks before returning her attention to the laces. "I was so like no one was ever. I thought you'd all leave us out there till kingdom come." Behind her the boy gently placed the guitar case in the back of the Rover. He took off his jacket, revealing a sweat-stained T-shirt. "This here's my brother, Lester," the girl said. "I'm Jenny. What's your name?"

"T Aloysius Walker," T said. "My business associates call me Tom Walker, my family and friends call me T, and no one at all calls me Aloysius, at least not to my face." He put the Rover in gear and pulled out onto the highway. "Where are we going?"

"Anywhere away from here," the boy said.

T saw that he was a good bit older than his first guess. "And where is here?" he asked.

"Tully. Tully, New York." Jen pulled off her boots, having at length finally unlaced them. "You don't mind, do you, T?" She held up a boot.

"Not at all. Make yourself comfortable."

Lester leaned into the front seat. "Where you headed, Tom?"

T feigned concern with a sixteen-wheeler roaring toward him in the passing lane. He considered whether or not to tell them the truth—that he was heading toward the region of the Thousand Islands, though not toward any specific location. Several hours earlier, after another long night of restless sleep, awakening to the prospect of yet another empty day in Salem, Virginia, he had packed a suitcase thoughtlessly, throwing in whatever clothes were readily available, thrown the suitcase into the back of the Rover along with his camera gear, and started for the Thousand Islands with the vague ambition of taking pictures there.

Once the truck had passed, he looked up into the rearview again and found Lester looking back at him. His eyes were dark and his arms were spread over the back seat in a position that accented his biceps, which were big enough not to need accenting.

"I'm just curious," T said. "What do you use on your hair?"

Lester took a strand of hair between his thumb and forefinger, as if to confirm the turn in the conversation. He had thick, shoulder-length auburn hair that was so obviously styled it would have made him look feminine if it weren't for the squared-off chin and cheekbones and the day's growth of beard. "What do I use on my hair?" he repeated.

Jen said, "Sometimes Lester spends more time on his hair than I do."

"That's bullshit." Lester looked up into the mirror. "My momma always said I had good hair. Ought to be proud of it."

"God bless her," Jen said. "That's just like her."

"She's a good woman," Lester said.

T nodded as if he were agreeing with something and then was quiet a while as he turned his attention back to the road, where the rolling hills of upstate New York slid slowly past while the sun continued falling toward the horizon. As if he might have an appointment, he glanced at the digital clock and temperature display on the dashboard. It was four o'clock, an unseasonably warm fall afternoon on the first Friday in October, 2002.

"Hey?" Jen broke the brief silence. She scratched his leg playfully with her toes. "Is it something we said?"

Lester added, "You're lookin' kind of down in the mouth there, bud."

"You did us the favor of a ride," Jen said. She jabbed at the air, as if an idea had just come to her. "We should cheer you up," she said. "We should have a party." She lifted herself slightly to look into the back seat. "Don't you think, Les?"

"Party down," Lester said.

T laughed, as if amused at the sudden rush of high spirits. "Where'd you two say you were from?" he asked. "You don't sound like you're from upstate New York."

"We're originally from Tennessee," Jen answered quickly. "Our family just moved up here a few years ago."

"Business move?" T asked. "Job?"

"You know," Les said, leaning into the front again, "you never did answer my first question."

"Which was?" T turned to find himself eye to eye with Lester. Up close, he smelled the faint ammoniac odor of sweat.

"Where you going? I asked you where you're going."

"Listen," T said to Jen, "I'm sorry if I looked glum." He touched her knee just for an instant, giving it a friendly pat.

Jen nudged Lester into the back seat and slid closer to T. She squeezed his thigh. "That's all right," she said. "We'll cheer you up."

"Where are you going, Ace?" Lester asked again.

Jen said, "Lighten up, Lester." She studied T's face a moment and then asked him gently, "Where are you heading, T?"

"Thousand Islands," T said.

"Jesus H . . ." Lester flung his head back, as if addressing the sky.

"I told you," Jen said, looking back. "I told you how things work. See?" She tucked her feet under her. "That's where we're going too," she said to T. "That's where we're trying to get to."

"So I guessed," he said.

"No, really," Jenny said. She grasped his arm and held it. "I have a relative's got a cabin there, by Alexandria Bay, and that's where we're trying to get to."

"That's amazing," T said. "Piece of luck."

"Shit." Jen turned to Lester. "He doesn't believe us."

Les spoke while yawning. "Who gives a fuck," he said, the words coming out high-pitched and distorted.

"You're a little out there," she said to T. "I've got a feeling about you," she added.

"Jenny," Lester said. He sounded sleepy. "Don't start fucking around."

T snuck a quick look into the back seat and saw that Lester had stretched out on his side. His eyes were closed and his head was resting on pressed-together hands like a little boy taking a nap. T said to Jenny, "Are you fucking around?"

She gave him a bemused smile. "Let's play a game," she said.

Les moaned and whispered something indiscernible.

"What kind of game?" T asked.

"This is how we play." She slid away from T, across the seat to the opposite side of the car, her feet still folded under her so that her knees were pointing at the steering wheel.

"Everybody gets to ask one question of somebody else, and that person has to tell the truth."

"That's so stupid," Lester said, his voice less sleepy. "How in hell we supposed to know he's telling the truth?"

"How's he supposed to know we're telling the truth?"

"Yeah," Lester said. "But we'll know if we are or aren't."

Jen closed her eyes as if she needed to be someplace different for just a moment.

T laughed.

"What?" Les sat up.

Jen said, "Try thinking about that for just a moment, Lester. Will you?" To T she said, "Play?"

T was in the passing lane behind a silver PT Cruiser, a car that looked to him as though it had been lifted from a cartoon strip. The Cruiser was attempting to pass a UPS truck by going approximately one mile per hour faster than the truck. He considered flashing his brights and then remembered he wasn't going anyplace and was in no rush to get there.

"Okay," he said. "How old are you?"

"Twenty-three," she shot back.

"You are not."

Les said, "She's playing the game. That's the truth."

"Really?" T said.

"There's got to be a little trust here," Jen said. "I swear, I'm twenty-three. You want me to prove it?"

She looked twenty-three like he looked seventy. She had a young girl's skin, unblemished by age: it vibrated good health;

it resonated youthful energy. On her face there wasn't as much as a crease other than the soft brackets around her mouth that came from smiling and talking. He looked at her again, at the full lips and striking green eyes, at the semicircle of her eyebrows, which were thick and full, not unlike the unruly profusion of blond hair that framed her face and fell to her shoulder. There seemed to be no excess fat on her anywhere: her thighs and legs were hard, her stomach taut under the fabric of her blouse. Even her feet in their thin white socks looked like a little girl's feet.

"Sorry," he said. "But I'm afraid I'll need some proof to believe you're twenty-three. If you'd told me you were seventeen, I wouldn't have blinked."

"Gee, Jen," Lester said. "Never heard that before, have you?"

"It's genetic," she said to T. "I'll always look a lot younger than I am. Mom's still like that." She reached into the rear seat and returned with a denim backpack that T was seeing for first time. Out of it she pulled a drawstring purse, Indian in design, maroon and decorated with elephants and multiarmed goddesses. She found a Tennessee driver's license in the purse and handed it to T.

T held the license in front of him, at the top of the steering wheel. *Cross, Jennifer. Born 10/02/79.* "Cross?" he said. "Does that say something about—"

"Don't even." She held up a hand like a stop sign. "I've heard every possible."

"And yesterday," T added. "Day before yesterday," he corrected himself. "Day before yesterday was your birthday?"

"All day," Jen said. "Well, technically, I wasn't born till five before midnight so, technically, about five minutes of day before yesterday."

"Did you have a party?"

Lester and Jenny both laughed. Jen said, "We're losing track of the game. My turn: How old are you?"

T glanced again at the picture on the driver's license. Even with flattened features and poor color reproduction, she looked good. Cut her hair and put her in a tasteful black dress and she'd turn heads at a gallery opening in Manhattan or a Broadway premier, the kind of events he had actually attended on occasion. "Fifty-seven," he said, and handed the license back to her.

"Now who's bullshitting who?" she said. "You're fifty-seven?"

"No shit," Les said. "I thought you were old, but fuck."

"You look forty-five, late forties top," Jen said. "And I'm usually pretty good at ages."

"Fifty-seven," T repeated. "Want to see my license?"

"No," she said. "Past twenty-five, guys don't lie about being older."

"What about women?"

"Past twenty-one."

"I'd be more flattered," T said, "if you asked to see my license, as if you absolutely just could not believe I was fifty-seven."

"I believe it," Les said, "now I look at you good."

"You're in great shape," Jen said. "Your stomach's flatter than Lester's."

"Only 'cause I drink too much beer," Lester said.

Jenny pushed her hair back and held it pressed to either side of her head under the heels of her hands. "You work out?" she asked.

"Used to go to the gym every day for many years," T said. "Lately I just walk and do calisthenics."

"Really? What kind of calisthenics?" She clasped her fingers in her hair and rolled her head gently side to side. "I try to work out every day, at least a little bit."

"This is fascinating," Lester said.

"You're just jealous," Jen answered.

Lester leaned into the front seat again. "It's my turn to ask a question." He folded his arms over the backrest. "T?" he said. "How much money you carrying with you?"

"Not much," T said. "A little over two hundred in my wallet. Mostly I use a pair of credit cards."

"Wouldn't be lying, would you? Guy dressed in a cashmere sweater looks like it cost a few hundred easy, haircut looks like a week's salary for a working man, driving a brand-new Land Rover that's, what, a fifty-thousand-dollar vehicle?"

"I have a Porsche at home."

"Really?"

"Absolutely."

"So you're worth some serious money."

T made a face suggesting that was at least partly true. He

said, "A lot less than I was worth about a year ago this time, which was when my divorce was finalized."

"Oh, yeah," Les said, as if sympathetic. "I bet."

"Do I get another question?" T asked Jen. She had turned solemn during Les's interrogation.

"Sure," she said. "Keep going."

"Hey, wait." Les put a hand on T's shoulder. "Slow down." He crouched and pointed out the window to an approaching overpass, where T could make out two figures looking out over the highway with something between them, resting on a railing. The sun was just above the horizon, a red ball sinking toward a long line of hills, turning the clouds pink and salmon and orange. They were on a straight stretch of 81, just beyond Syracuse, heading for the Canadian border.

T slowed down. "You want me to pull off the road?"

"No. Just watch those two on the bridge. What's that between them?"

T's eyesight wasn't what it used to be. The people on the overpass appeared to be leaning on the railing and looking out over the highway the way someone might sit back against a rock and peer out over the ocean. A beautiful day was coming to an end. He assumed he was approaching two people talking while they looked out at the hills and the long stretch of road. "What about them?" he asked Lester.

"Just watch what they got between them there."

"It's a baby." Jen fell back into her seat. "Pair of morons, putting a baby up there like that."

"Jesus, you're right," Lester said.

"Don't worry, Les," she added. "I don't think they'll drop a baby on us."

"These days . . ." he said.

T had to wait another few seconds before he could finally make out what Les and Jen were talking about. There, on the overpass, was a baby strapped into what appeared to be a car seat, with a young woman holding the car seat on one side and a young man holding it on the other. The baby stared off happily at the hills while the two people faced each other over the infant. After he passed under the bridge he checked the rearview and saw a car pulled off the road on the other side of the overpass. "Kid was probably driving them crazy crying," he said.

"You think they'd throw it onto the highway?" Les asked, as if suddenly frightened.

T and Jenny both laughed at the notion.

"What's so funny?"

"You," Jen said. "You're a screaming paranoiac, I've told you that."

"Why? He just said—"

"It probably calms the baby looking at the cars going by. For God's sake." Jen looked at T as if searching for commiseration. "Throw the baby off the bridge . . ."

"If I'm a little paranoid, Jen," Lester said, "it's not like I don't have reason."

"Point," she said.

"So my question—" T allowed himself a dramatic pause.

For reasons he fully grasped, he decided that he was actually at this point enjoying himself, though *enjoying* wasn't the right word. If there was indeed a right word for what he was feeling, he didn't know it. It would have to denote the pleasure one felt at the prospect of being engaged in any human activity with the potential to surprise as well as the potential to elicit real human feelings, even if the elicited feelings were potentially going to be very bad; especially, the word would suggest, after a long period of emotional isolation, or of emotional repression, or, simply, after a long period of emptiness, a period devoid of genuine human contact and intimacy. *The pleasure at anticipating something exciting about to happen involving other human beings.* Something like that. *A species of exhilaration.* "Is this," he continued after his pause, "something you two do on a regular basis: random hitchhiking and robbery?"

"Who said anything about robbery?" Lester said.

Jennifer said, "We told you where we're going. We're going to the Thousand Islands."

"Yes, that's what you told me. But you were lying. Just as you're lying about Lester here being your brother."

"This guy's sharp," Lester said.

"Shut up, Les." Jen stretched her legs across the seat so that her foot touched T's thigh. "You want to know the truth? Play the game. Ask us direct questions."

"All right," T said. "Lester is not your brother, is he?"

"No. He's not."

"Who is he?"

"Ex-lover. Past mistake. He appears out of nowhere—what? three days ago now?—having totally screwed up his own life and needing, apparently, to screw up mine too."

"Jesus, Jenny," Lester said. "How many times—"

"Be quiet, Lester." Jenny pulled her hair away from her eyes. "Really," she said. "Just be quiet back there. Let me play this game with T, okay? It's amusing me."

"Fine," Lester said. "Play."

"My turn," she said. "Do you really own a Porsche?"

"Yes. Bought it new last year."

"And you really are wealthy?"

"How do you define wealthy?"

"A million or so, that you have access to, pretty easily."

"Yes, then, I'm wealthy, though I have to add, as a caveat, that's a pretty meager definition of wealth."

"Obviously," she said, "we're from different backgrounds."

"Obviously," he said. "My turn. Do you plan on robbing me?"

"Right now?" she said. "This moment?"

"At any moment, from the time I stopped for you till now."

"That's not easy to answer directly."

"Why not?"

"Because—" She pulled her foot away from his thigh, tucking her feet under her again. She crossed her arms beneath her breasts as if trying to hug and fold herself into as small a space as possible. "Because," she continued, "though the plan was to rob you, I wasn't ever really sure I'd actually let Lester go through with it."

"Just out of curiosity," T said, "what exactly was the plan?"

"I play like a hooker," she said. "Which I'm not nor have I ever been, for the record. But I come on like a country tramp or a hooker or whatever once I figure you out; then I offer to go in the back seat with you while Lester drives."

"And this is something you've done before?" T asked.

"No. It's not. Though I think Lester here might have some similar past experiences. Lester?"

Lester didn't answer. He leaned back in his seat with his arms spread out grasping the backrest to either side of him.

"Then what?" T pressed. "Once I get in the back seat with you?"

"You don't make it to the back seat. Before you get there, Lester hits you over the head with a piece of pipe he's got stuck down the back of his pants."

"That's great, Jen," Lester said, breaking his silence but not moving. "Thanks for taking away the element of surprise. What am I supposed to do now, hit him over the head while he's driving?"

"Why don't we drop the whole hitting-over-the-head thing?" T said. "It won't be necessary. I already planned on taking you wherever you want to go."

"Really?" Les said. "And did you plan on giving us your car and your money?"

When T didn't answer, the Rover filled up with a silence that felt pressurized, as if it were pushing against the windows and doors. The vehicle continued rolling on, and Jennifer continued to sit with her feet folded under her, holding herself in her own arms, though she had turned to look out the front window and appeared to be quietly watching the sky as the last light faded and the somber clouds deepened toward darkness. T held the steering wheel with both hands and watched the road. Behind him, he could feel Lester's presence where he occupied the whole of the back seat as if it were his throne. He hit a button and opened his window a crack to let in some fresh air, but the roar of wind was so loud he closed it again immediately. Jennifer sighed, as if saddened by the whole situation. She let her head fall back against the headrest. T noticed for the first time the slightest whiff of perfume. It was a faintly sweet odor that he both smelled and felt distinctly on the tip of his tongue. It was strange that he hadn't noticed it before, as if the sense of smell were somehow enhanced by silence. When he saw, glancing at her, that she had closed her eyes, he took the chance to look more closely. Unquestionable that she was beautiful physically, with the allure of youth and lucky proportions: a narrow waist, full breasts, a sleek frame . . . But there was something else about her, something he could see more clearly through the silence, something in the cast of her face, in the way her lips were parted as if she were full of words waiting to be spoken. It made him want to touch her face, and when he found himself imagining how soft her skin would be, he turned away and pushed his thoughts back to the road.

The stillness lasted for a full forty-five minutes, a space of time that felt at points like eternity. It grew dark. He turned on

the lights. The surrounding hills and farms disappeared and
were replaced by the nothing of darkness. The stars came out.
They were more than an hour past Syracuse, having just
passed Watertown, which would be the last urban center of
any size in the U.S. They were approximately another hour
from the Thousand Islands and the Canadian border, with
nothing in front of them but farm land and marsh and eleven
hours of night. T worked on a sentence in his mind. *It seems to
me,* he thought of saying, *that we'll need to make a decision.* But
as soon as the sentence was fully formed, he rejected it as too
dramatic. What he really wanted to say was something very
simple, like: *Okay. So what are you going to do?* But he also
wanted to inject into that question some rhetorical method of
developing an argument to dissuade Lester from answering
him with a pipe over the back of his head. He wanted to ask
them what they were going to do and he also wanted to argue
against anything that included serious injury to the driver, and
he was having trouble finding a rhetorical tack that didn't
sound wimpy or desperate or, on the other hand, ridiculously
nonchalant, as if it didn't really matter to him at all what they
decided—though, strangely, that was probably the closest to
what he actually felt.

He kept driving, figuring that someone at some point was
bound to say or do something. He had spent most of the past
year alone and doing nothing in Salem, Virginia, where after
more than half a century of life, he found himself isolated,
trapped in an indolence that manifested itself through addic-
tions to computer games, chess, jazz, and good wine. The chess,

jazz, and good wine were at least somewhat socially acceptable. The computer games he kept secret. Now at least he was interested. He was interested in what might happen next.

"All right," Jenny said, as if only a moment had passed since the conversation had come to a halt. "Look," she said to Lester, "we're not robbing this guy. Period. Okay?"

"Thank you," T said. "I appreciate that."

"Shut up," Lester said. To Jenny he added, "What do you mean we're not robbing him? What the fuck are we doing then?"

"I don't know."

T said, "May I make a suggestion?"

"What you may do is shut the fuck up," Lester said. "What you may do is just be quiet before I cave your skull in just for the hell of it."

Jenny said, "Oh for Christ's sake, Lester."

"What?" he yelled, the word percussive and loud as a gunshot.

"What?" she shouted back at him, jumping to her knees. "What?" she screamed again, this time throwing a punch at his face, which T in the rearview saw him ward off by covering his head with his forearms. "Don't you fuckin' scream at me!"

"Jenny," he said from behind his arms.

"What? What, Lester? What do you want to say to me?"

T guessed Jenny was five-five, maybe a little shorter, but knotted up the way she was, clenched and tight and sinewy, he imagined she could throw a substantial punch.

"Jenny," Lester repeated. "Calm down."

"Who shouted first, Lester? Who brought out the big-bad-bully voice, Lester?"

"Jenny," he said.

"What?"

"Jenny, we have to deal with this guy. If we don't take him off; if *I* don't take him off, what are we going to do?"

"That's a good question," she said. "Are you done screaming at us? Are you done cavin' people's skulls in?"

He didn't answer. He took his hands away from his face but continued to lean back and away from her.

She said, "I asked you a question, Lester."

"Do you want me to be done?" he said. "Because I don't know what the hell you're really thinking, Jen."

"I'm thinking you should be quiet is what I'm really thinking."

"Okay, fine," he said. "You want me to be quiet, fine." He slid away from her, positioning himself out of T's sight, directly behind the driver's seat. "Because I'm sorry about all this," he added. "But what the fuck are we supposed to do with no money and no car in the middle of fuckin' nowhere except rip off somebody?"

"So are you done now?" she said. "Are you going to be quiet?"

"Fine, quiet. But we've got no money. Not a cent."

Jenny was still a moment, as if testing to see if Lester were really through talking. When they had driven a while in the dark and silence, she continued, "So, as I was saying, the plan was to rob you, but I don't think it was ever really going to happen. I'm not really violent, and I'm not a thief."

T said, "You're not violent and you're not a thief, but you were planning to knock me unconscious and steal my car and my money. Is that right?"

"That's about right," Lester's voice came out of the back seat. "It was my plan."

"I'd feel more guilty about it," Jennifer added, "except, as I said, I don't think you were ever in any real danger."

As I said . . . T noted the use of the grammatically more formal *as* rather than the typical *like*. He also noted that her slight Southern lilt had almost completely disappeared. He said, "You're becoming downright enigmatic, Jennifer."

"I'm a girl dressed in skin-tight red leather pants with her blouse half open. I would think that's pretty easy to interpret."

"A girl dressed in red leather pants with her blouse half open who says *as I said* rather than *like I said;* who knows what *enigmatic* means; and who came into the car with a country Southern accent and a full-tilt airhead act—*My feeet are juust kiillin' me!*—and who, an hour and a half later, sounds more like she's from northern Virginia than Opelousas, Louisiana, and is beginning to sound like she might even have some higher education."

Lester said, laying on the accent, "I got fahmily in Opelousas, dude."

"All right, so," Jennifer said, "if we're not exactly what we seem—what about you? You stopped for a girl dressed like a whore and a seedy-looking guy in a black leather jacket—"

"Thank you," Lester interrupted. "Very nice."

"What are we supposed to think of you?" Jen finished.

"That I'm stupid?" T said. "Or reckless?"

Lester added, "Or a just a horny old man."

"Want to know what I'm thinking?" Jennifer said. "I'm considering the possibility that you're majorly fucked up."

"Majorly fucked up?" T said. "Could you be more precise?"

She shook her head. "It's getting late," she said. "And you have no idea how tired I am."

When T was in his late twenties, living in Manhattan, his life wrapped up as it would be for another twenty-plus years in the development of his businesses, he had taken a late-night drive east, out to the island, heading nowhere in particular, as was his wont when he was stressed and tense, though probably better to say overly stressed and tense since stressed and tense was pretty much the normal state of affairs at that time. He was a man whose idea of a great day in the city was to spend an afternoon wandering through MOMA or the Met or the Guggenheim, followed by dinner somewhere nice and a play that people were talking about, something like Albee's *The Play About the Baby* or a new production of Chekhov; and at that time he was married to a woman who thought his interest in art was pretentious, who once actually laughed at him when he told her he dreamed of being a photographer and showing his pictures in the downtown galleries. Given that he didn't even own a decent camera at the time, it wasn't hard to understand why his admission elicited a quick, spontaneous laugh. It hurt nonetheless, and he still remembered the moment vividly, as was also his wont, to protect and nurture wounds for a lifetime. He was married to the wrong woman and would be for a few more years; he was spending the bulk of his life developing maintenance, house-and-office-cleaning, and restoration businesses that were of no interest to him beyond the large sums of money he was coaxing them to generate; he was edgy and anxious all the time; and during this aimless, calming ride out on the island he came upon two girls hitchhiking on an almost deserted back road.

He stopped for them, of course, though he couldn't see much in the dark beyond that they looked like girls, small of frame, with long hair and delicate features. After he pulled over, they both got in the back seat without a word, just opened the door and got in the back seat, so that he had to turn around and look before he understood that he had just picked up two very drunk, barely teenaged girls. They looked back at him with wide eyes and dopey smiles. "Ladies?" he said. "Where would you like to go?" They giggled in response. For a moment he thought they might be drugged out on acid or who knew what, maybe one of the designer psychedelics that were popular with teens those days, but the smell of whiskey on their breath cleared up that question quickly as it began to suffuse the closed atmosphere of the car. He looked them over more closely and saw they might not even be teenagers. Their small breasts might not just be small, they might be still developing. Their shortness of stature might not just be shortness, they might still be growing. But clearly they were two very young girls, drunk in the back seat of his car. He mustered the most benevolent and avuncular of smiles. "Ladies," he repeated gently, "you've been drinking." Which brought on more giggles. "Would you like me to deliver you someplace?"

"Not really," the one on the right said. "We don't really have anyplace to go."

The one on the left smiled coyly and said, "Have you ever been in the back seat of your own car?"

The one on the right added, "It's cozy back here."

T had never doubted the moral correctness of what he had done at that point, which was to get out of the car, open the back door, lead them one at a time out onto the dark road, and leave them where he had found them. Chances were slim that another car would pass before they sobered up and made their way back to their respective homes, which were almost certainly in one of the nearby developments. It was very late. The area was remote. The road was lightly used, even during the day. He had never considered even for a second doing anything else but escorting those two girls out of his car. That was real. That was something that had happened in the real world, and he had revisited the incident often during the endless months of disgrace preceding his banishment, and it came to mind again as he drove through the dark, some thirty years later, with two new hitchhikers in his car.

"Help me out here," he said to Jennifer. "Forget about me,

whether I'm majorly fucked up. What about you two? You're not kids. This isn't a joyride. What are you thinking? You rob my car and take my money, then what? You risk several years in jail for a few hundred bucks and a ride? That doesn't make sense. What are you thinking?"

Jen said, "You're being far too rational."

Lester added, "Via circumstances beyond your control, you find yourself with no money, no transportation, and your life in danger if you don't immediately get very far away from where you are. What would you do, Tom?"

"Your life in danger?"

"I bet you—" Jenny said to Lester. "I'll bet you he wouldn't go and put the only friend he's got in mortal danger with him."

"Jesus Christ, Jenny— If I could take it back—"

"Yes, but you can't," she said. "Here we are." To T, she said, "Look," and then paused as if collecting her thoughts. She seemed changed again, as if several layers of masks had fallen away and the real person smoldering under the pretense was burning closer to the surface. "Look," she repeated. "You said you'd take us to the Thousand Islands. I wasn't lying. We really are trying to get there." She dug into her bag and came out with a scrap of blue-lined yellow paper, which she put on the dashboard in front of him. "This is where we're going," she said, indicating an address handwritten on the paper in red pen. "If you'd just take us there, I promise: we'll say good-bye. We'll be out of your life."

"I'll take you," T said, without bothering to look at the address. "I said I'd take you where you're going."

"Thank you," she said, and she straightened herself out in her seat, stretched out her legs, buttoned up her blouse, laid her head back and closed her eyes, as if to say, *Okay. I'm done. Bullshit's over.*

Lester leaned forward out of the shadows of the back seat and wordlessly dropped a lead pipe alongside T's thigh. Then he lay down out of sight.

A moment later they were both sleeping soundly, and T realized how exhausted they must have been all along. Jenny had closed her eyes and literally a few seconds later her face went slack and her body relaxed into the seat and her chest rose and fell in a regular pattern of deep breaths. In the back seat, Lester moaned, making a sound so embarrassingly and unguardedly sexual that he had to be deep in sleep. A moment later he did it again, only this time it was a mix of sexual pleasure and agony; then with his next breath he groaned yet again, and that final time it was all suffering, the kind of sound someone might make after learning of an irrevocable loss. Then they were both still and the only sound in the car was the whisper of their breath as they slept.

They weren't far from Alexandria Bay, a place T hadn't seen in more than thirty years, since his college days at Syracuse University, where he had been a terrible student, cutting more classes than he attended before miraculously managing to graduate with a C average and a degree in English. That he had managed only thanks to a professor who in effect gifted him with twelve credits for independent studies he had never taken: Professor Carolyn Wald, an immensely proper-looking woman in her fifties, with whom he used to smoke pot, have sex, and go fishing off Lake Ontario and sometimes in the Thousand Islands around Alexandria Bay. She taught English literature, specializing in the Romantic poets, and she would sometimes recite poems to him from memory while they fished. He'd been thinking about her a good bit these days too, and he suspected her memory—she was long dead, of cancer—had something to do with his choice of the Thousand Islands as a destination once he had decided on this spontaneous trip.

He spent a lot of time lately reviewing the whole career of his sex life, which he reasoned was understandable, given what had happened to him, given the place where he arrived early one evening when a indignant young woman slapped him across the face in disgust. Police had arrived at his Long Island home in a dozen official vehicles, all with brightly colored, flashing, revolving, strobing lights that turned the quiet dusk of his street into a carnival—which was what the whole thing was designed to be, a carnival sideshow, meant to attract attention, meant as a warning to others. They came in early evening, when the daylight was just beginning to fade, when all his neighbors were home, the families gathered around the evening meal. He had just finished dinner and was about to watch the news. From the place where he sat in his flung-back leather recliner, he could see the police cars through the living room's bay window. They lined the curb in front of his house and pulled into his driveway, and still it didn't occur to him for even a second that he was the one they were coming for. When what seemed like a small army of police piled out of the various cars and vans and four officers—two men, two women; two in uniform, two in street clothes—walked up his blacktop driveway and along the red-brick path to his front door, he assumed they were looking for someone in the neighborhood and wanted to ask him if he knew this person or that one, or had he seen this person or that one, and he was only slightly alarmed that all four officers had their guns drawn.

His wife wasn't home. She had a convenient dinner engagement in the city. He opened the front door and a uniformed officer opened the screen door simultaneously; someone asked him his name—*Yes, Thomas Walker*—and then everything started to go very fast: someone grabbed him roughly by the arm, someone read him his rights, someone yanked his wrists behind him and put him in handcuffs. All the while, once all this started happening, he was laughing. He kept saying, *Wait. This is obviously a mistake,* and he laughed good-humoredly, as if he understood how embarrassed they were all going to be when they discovered their error, whatever it was, that they had the wrong Thomas Walker or whatever, since they could not possibly be sending a tiny army of police to arrest him, this Thomas Walker, who hadn't done anything seriously illegal since his pot-smoking days as a college student.

If they really did tell him why he was being arrested, as they later claimed in court, he never heard it. He refused counsel. He asked them to recheck the name, address, and age of this Thomas Walker they were after. He knew it was all a mistake and continued working with that assumption even after they carried his computer and monitor into the barren little room where he was seated behind a pitted wooden conference table; even after they plugged it in and booted it up and clicked through the image files till they came to a pornographic image and asked him if he had downloaded it from the Internet, and did he understand that it was a crime in the state of New York to possess child pornography. As he looked hard at the picture on the screen it began slowly and terrifyingly to sink in that it wasn't a mistake at all, that he was indeed the man they had come to arrest.

The quiet in the little room at that moment was extraordinary. He wasn't breathing, nor, it seemed, was anyone else. There were no uniformed officers present. The detective across from him, on the right of the computer, was probably in his forties, though he looked older, with bags under his eyes and developing jowls and graying hair combed over the center of his head where the hair had thinned to balding. An unattractive young woman, probably in her early thirties, leaned over the table on the other side of the computer. She was stick-figure thin, and her clothes—K-mart-quality blue slacks and maroon blouse—flopped around the bony projections of her shoulders, elbows, and knees. She was the one asking the questions while the others watched intently. It was as if somehow everyone understood that he was just then comprehending the situation.

He studied the picture on the monitor. In a cheap, wood-paneled room that suggested the interior of a trailer in the closeness of its space, a pale-skinned older woman lay on a faded green sofa holding a young girl gently in her arms. He'd guess the woman was in her forties. The girl, though fully developed, was clearly very young. She might not yet have even reached her teens. They were both without clothes. Most of the woman's body was covered by the girl's. On the woman's face was a benevolent, loving, motherly expression. She held the girl in a protecting embrace, one hand smoothing the girl's hair, the other wrapped around her back, holding her shoulder. The girl's cheek was pressed between the woman's breasts. Her eyes were closed and her mouth was open in an expression of sexual ecstasy, the kind of look a woman might have in the moment before climax. The older woman's face and body were not unattractive, only worn by age. Her skin was slack and pale, furrowed with creases and lines and splotched here and there with mild discolorations. The girl in her arms was still perfect. Her skin was vibrant, her breasts full, her face utterly unmarked by time or experience. Her body seemed to glow in that woman's arms as, in the bottom left foreground of the picture, seen only from the back and side, a man hunched over slightly in the act of penetrating the girl as the woman held her, and the girl pressed her cheek into the woman's breast and opened her mouth in that moan almost audible in the picture. The hirsute body of the man was bulky and thick, bear-like in its partial crouch. He looked to be of an age with the woman, though his face wasn't visible, only his body, the bulk of it weighing down the bottom of the picture, his erection sliding into the downy hair that filled the perfect V between the girl's legs.

The stick-figure woman asked the question again: Was he aware that it was a crime in the state of New York to possess child pornography?

T looked up from the picture to the woman asking the question. His arms and legs were shaking slightly. His stomach roiled. He said, "I didn't do anything."

The woman, her voice rising, answered, "You downloaded a picture of a child being raped. You kept it on your computer."

T said, "But it was already there."

"On your computer?" she said, incredulous.

"On the Internet."

"But you downloaded it to your computer," she said. "You looked at it with lust, for sexual pleasure."

"With interest," T said.

"Interest?" she said. "What do you mean, interest?"

"I mean the picture is interesting," T said.

"Interesting?" She looked horrified. "Interesting?" she repeated. "This is a child being raped, and you think it's"—her hand shot out and she slapped him hard across the cheek—"interesting?"

The slap was hard enough to knock him back in his seat and leave the imprint of her hand on his face, but at the time he hardly felt it. It was as if his body had gone numb. He wanted to explain himself to the woman who had slapped him and he was too busy trying to formulate the words to pay much attention to the physical blow. The other detectives had been shocked by the slap; he had seen it on their faces for a brief moment before they gathered themselves back to professional impassivity, as if there were nothing surprising at all in what had just happened. T wanted to direct the woman's attention back to the picture. Look, he wanted to say. She's not being raped. She's been seduced by the older woman and given as a gift, an offering to the man's desire. Look at the motherly tenderness in the older woman's eyes, the way the young girl holds on to her, as if for reassurance. She's been seduced. She's been seduced by the older woman and delivered into the arena of sex. It's terrible, I know, he wanted to say. In the real world, it's terrible. But this is a picture. I was fascinated by a picture. I wasn't sanctioning what happened, I was looking at an image. There's a difference, he wanted to say. There's an important difference. In the real world, it's terrible, it's a crime; but this is an image, a powerful, troubling, resonant image that reaches someplace deep and disturbing. I was interested in the image; I wasn't sanctioning the act. I didn't *do* anything, he wanted to say, except look at a picture.

But he never got to say any of it. Instead he watched the stick-figure woman as she went to a countertop sink in a corner and washed her hands, and then looked back at him one more time with loathing before leaving the room.

In the dark and quiet of the Rover, approaching Alexandria Bay, T drew in a deep, calming breath and tried to empty his mind. His muscles were knotted and stiff. He felt a headache coming on. Alongside him, Jenny was stretched out with her head close to his thigh, her knees bent and her body hunched and cramped into an uncomfortable-looking S. He ran his fingers along a lock of her hair and could almost taste the texture of its silky waves. He moved the lead pipe away from her head, to the floor by her feet. She stirred with his movements and turned onto her back with her knees up in the air and her forehead jammed into the space between his thigh and the back of the seat.

Driving through the night, with Jenny and Lester sleeping, he thought of his own daughter, of family trips with her and her stepbrother sleeping buckled up in the back seat and Alicia, his wife, his daughter's stepmother, sleeping trustingly alongside him. There were few things in this life that he liked better than driving at night with his family asleep around him—though even the memory of those moments seemed to come to him from another lifetime, from some other dimension of existence, one he had passed through in a dream before finding himself utterly different, in the current moment, at night, in a strange vehicle with a girl in red leather pants curled up where Alicia should be, and a man in the back seat instead of Evan, his stepson, whom he had raised from the age of two and whom he loved dearly and from whom he was now irrevocably separated, as he was separated from his own daughter, Maura, from his first marriage, who was herself now married and living in London and had a daughter of her own, whom she had painfully explained to him he could not under any circumstances ever be alone with, breaking his heart, reducing him to tears in her sight before she even finished speaking. Not that any of it mattered; not that he had seen any of them in more than a year; now he was this other person, this other T Walker, leading this other, until recently, vacuous life.

By the time he exited Route 81 for Alexandria Bay, his palms were sweaty, he was nauseous, his skin was clammy, and he had a roaring headache. He picked up the scrap of yellow paper from the dash. The address read, "Cabin 12, Wolf Point." He put the paper in his pocket and headed for a gas station just beyond the exit, where he could already see the figure of an old man hunched over some kind of reading material behind a plate-glass window. In the back seat, Lester moaned softly and started to snore.

B y the time he found the cabin and peered in through grimy windows to the dark interior, it was almost eight. The old guy at the gas station had given him easy directions before asking if he was a friend of Chuck's, to which T had nodded and said, "Chuck's a buddy from way back," and then popped two Advil and washed them down with a swig from an eight-ounce Perrier, which he had been delighted to find beside the various columns of brightly colored soft drinks. "Haven't seen him in some time," the old man said. "He's fine," T answered, "been busy," and he pushed the remaining Perrier and a six-pack of Coke and the opened Advil bottle toward the cash register. "Let me have the big bucket of that fried chicken too," he said, and pointed to the countertop glass case of chicken pieces on racks under heat lamps. Then he paid for the gas and supplies and left with the red-and-white bucket of chicken under his arm and a plastic bag with the drinks in hand.

Wolf Point turned out to be a long scrap of rugged shore pushing out into the Saint Lawrence. It was lined with red-wood cabins. T had parked the Rover under the wide, rambling crown of an oak tree and waited a moment to see if either of his hitchhikers would stir once the sound of the engine ceased and the loud silence of this still, dark place filled the car. They didn't. Which wasn't surprising, given that neither had stirred through the pumping of the gas and the exiting and entering and the dropping of the chicken and soft drinks on the car floor. If even the thick, greasy smell of Southern-fried chicken failed to wake them, no reason to be surprised that the swell of silence didn't penetrate their sleep either. He took the black Mag light from the glove compartment, left them sleeping in the car, and climbed a hill to the cabins, all of which appeared to be empty. There were no cars in sight, no vehicles of any kind, only a grassy slope of land mostly hidden by darkness, and the moonlit outline of cabins against the sky.

The land fell off precipitously behind the first cabin, dropping several feet to the water. The buildings were close together in a zigzagging line that proceeded up a hill. He pointed the flashlight at a door, found the number 1 carved into the wood frame, and switched the light off before following a grassy trail from cabin to cabin until he reached the last one, with the number 12 on the door. It was the largest of the group, on the tip of the peninsula, on a rocky promontory a good twenty feet above the water. He searched the interior through several dirty windows, moving the beam of light over the walls and floor, and was surprised to find the place comfortably furnished with rustic chairs and tables. There were two small bedrooms and one large one, with a mahogany sleigh bed and a black bearskin rug—the real thing, head and all—atop a larger plush white rug in front of a brick fireplace. Clearly, no one had been inside in some time. The surfaces were all covered with dust, the windows were grimy, and the kitchen counters were speckled with what looked like mouse droppings. He checked the front and back door and, finding them both locked, returned to the Rover, where Lester and Jenny were still sleeping soundly.

The temperature was dropping, but it was still a mild, summery night. He sat on the front bumper of the Rover in the dark and looked out over the Saint Lawrence as the rising moon cast its path of light over the purple-black river. Wind rustled through trees. He considered whether or not to wake Jenny and Lester, having delivered them, as promised, to the address scrawled he assumed in Jenny's hand on Jenny's scrap of paper. He had his own housing for the night yet to worry about, not to mention the still live possibility of being beaten and robbed and for all he knew murdered and dumped in the river. They still needed his car. They still needed his money. With that thought, he went back into the Rover and retrieved the length of pipe from the floor, where it lay alongside

Jenny's purse. The interior light went on with the opening of the door, and he watched them both a moment to see if either would stir. Neither did. Lester lay on his stomach as if he were trying to wedge himself into the seam where the backrest and cushions met. Jenny lay on her back, fully stretched out across the seat, with one arm flung over her eyes and the other dangling to the floorboards, her fingers resting on the six-pack of Coke. Her blouse had pulled loose from her pants, leaving a six-inch swath of skin exposed under the bright interior light as if magnified. Between the straight line of red leather low on her hips and the pulled-back, silky fabric of the blouse, her bare skin soaked up the light. He was tempted to touch her there, to lay his hand against her belly, but he stuck the Mag light back in the glove compartment, retreated with the pipe, and closed the car door, not gently; when again neither of them moved, he tossed the pipe into the woods and started down toward the rocky inlet at the foot of the peninsula.

Close to the water he found an outcropping protected from the wind. Behind him in the moonlight, he could see the Rover parked under the oak tree's umbrella of branches. In front of him, the river, and now a long black cargo vessel of some sort sliding into sight, coming out of the Atlantic heading west. He and Carolyn had once almost been killed by such a vessel. They had been fishing for hours, talking easily about politics and history and literature, with Carolyn doing most of the talking while T mostly listened avidly and threw in a comment here and there, but mostly he was enjoying the listening; then, for no reason, he looked behind him and saw a black wall of steel bearing down on their fourteen-foot jon boat, which, compared to the leviathan looming over them, was as tiny as an insect. He managed to sputter out Carolyn's name before nearly capsizing the boat as he scurried to the bow, where Carolyn was absorbed in watching the thin yellow filament of her fishing line. They laughed about that later, what he could have been thinking as he tried to run away from an ocean-going cargo ship by moving from the stern to the bow of their little jon boat. Carolyn, luckily, was more self-possessed. She started the outboard with a single hard yank of the engine cord and piloted the little boat out of the path of the ship with seconds to spare, the rush of water from the prow actually lifting them up and pushing them away from the more dangerous waters in its wake.

T was older now than Carolyn had been then, though not a lot older. She never had told him her exact age while they were together. It was only after she died and her obituary was written up in the alumni magazine that he figured out she had been in her early fifties during the college years of their affair, an affair that kept going on and off right up until a few days before he married Brooke, when Carolyn would have been fifty-seven, his age at the very moment, a moment in which he was looking out at the Saint Lawrence on a mild October night, gazing at a river full of memories of her. She was an extraordinary woman: brilliant, funny, compassionate, sexual, daring, loving. She knew she risked everything in having an affair with him. "An undergraduate!" she would say. "My God! Am I crazy?" She made him laugh. He was a long-haired kid posturing as a poet and artist, which was an amazingly common pose for the time. She was a poet and a scholar who knew everything there was to know about William Butler Yeats, and a lot of what there was to know about everything else. He wore sandals and jeans and wrinkled Ts in summer, and boots and jeans and wrinkled flannel shirts in winter. He went unshaven for days, occasionally grew a beard, and always looked ragged. She wore pressed khaki slacks and starched colored blouses, and always looked neat and well groomed. People who saw them together off campus assumed mother and wayward son. On campus, professor and student. No one would have dreamed they were lovers. Secrecy was the affair's admission price. She had made that very clear, and though he would have loved to advertise to his handful of friends the fact that he was sleeping with one of the school's most respected professors, he didn't. He kept the secret all his life. Not his wives or children or friends, no one knew, then or now. Looking out at the river and remembering Carolyn Wald was like looking into himself and remembering a secret.

After his arrest in September 2000, he had spent several more months in New York while his life unraveled—*exploded* is more accurate, it happened with such rapidity—and then moved to Salem, Virginia, after initialing a series of complex legal agreements by which he avoided incarceration; and after only a few weeks in his new home, Islamic terrorists flew two passenger planes into the World Trade Center's twin towers. His first wife, Brooke, called him at 8:30 in the morning on September 11, waking him from a sound sleep. Brooke had always been unpredictable. A short, plump woman with limp brown hair and a pudgy face, she possessed an impressive intellect that seemed to do nothing but cause her trouble. She spent half her life going back and forth between therapists and doctors, and he spent most of his life with her waiting for whatever erratic and disruptive thing she'd do next. He had reconnected with her in the most intense period of publicity soon after the arrest. She had never stopped feeling guilty about walking out on him and their daughter a few days before Maura's fifth birthday, simply disappearing one day and leaving him to figure out what the hell had happened. Reentering his life during a period when no one else wanted anything to do with him was her way of making amends. He appreciated it and probably talked to her more during those few months than in all the years of their marriage, so when she called that morning he was only mildly surprised.

"Are you watching this?" she said.

"What?" he said. "Watching what?" He was standing at the kitchen counter in his pajamas, looking out a bay window at the foothills of the Blue Ridge Mountains aflame in fall red and orange. It was a beautiful autumn day, the sky a clear, crisp blue. "I was sleeping," he said.

She said, "Turn on the television. We're under attack."

T's first assumption was that Brooke had gone off her medication and was in the midst of another crisis. He turned on the television and there were the gleaming facades of the twin towers majestic against the same crisp and clear blue sky he saw out of his own kitchen window, the top of the north tower blackened by smoke spilling out of an ugly gash. He put the phone down on the coffee table, not realizing he was hanging up on Brooke. He was in Salem, Virginia, a part of the world he had never even heard of until one of his lawyers had recommended it as a place where he might retreat and regroup and incidentally honor his legally binding promise to move out of New York. He was in Salem, Virginia, watching a televised attack on New York, with everyone he had ever loved far away from him or gone forever. Then, it seemed, he spent the next several months in front of the television set—the months of the anthrax attacks and the Afghan war—and during all that time he found himself thinking again and again of Carolyn Wald reading him poems as they floated along riverways lined with high weeds, listening to catbirds and sparrows while they fished for bass and pike and she read him her favorite poems by Hopkins and Yeats, Dickinson and Roethke and Stevens and scores of poets whose names he no longer remembered.

Her favorite Yeats poem was "The Second Coming," and the first time she had read it to him was at the very beginning of the affair. She had a house in the Syracuse countryside, a big, lovely, sprawling home three times the size any one person might need, filled with art and antiques and wall upon wall of hardcover books. On weekends she often had students out to the house for dinner parties, and it was after one of those parties, on a snowy winter night in front of her fireplace, on a soft-textured, thick-piled rug, that she had knelt over him and placed the flat of her hands on his chest while he was lying on his back watching the flames sputter and jump, everyone else gone, only the two of them in the house. She recited the opening lines of the poem and he offered her a pleasant smile in return, as if amused but really not knowing what to make of her behavior. She was his professor. He was half in love with her, in the way students fall in love with professors they both like and admire and who engagingly return their affection. He was twenty, in the midst of the third literature course he had taken with her, a veteran of a dozen of her dinner parties, the student who came early to help prepare and stayed late to help clean up. From the spot where he lay comfortably by the hearth, he could see the fire to the left of him, and to the right, through a bay window, snow floating fat and thick, bright flakes drifting down through the beam of an exterior light. She pushed his hair away from his eyes and recited the poem as she undid the buttons of his shirt and pushed his undershirt up to lay her hands flat against the hard muscles of his chest. "Things fall apart," she said, and crossed her arms to grasp the bottom of her sweater and pull it off over her head, tousling her hair. She kissed him on the mouth then and proceeded to remove his clothes and her own and to make love to him there in front of the fire, without him ever moving off his back from the moment she lowered herself over him to the moment she fell against his chest, the top of her head under his chin. He held her against him, running his fingers over the waves of her spine, and innocently whispered that he loved her.

In front of him, on the water, the big cargo ship slipped out of sight.

"That you?" Jenny's voice came from behind T.

He jumped, but probably not enough for her to notice in the dark. She stood above him on a narrow ledge of rock, her arms thrust out like a tightrope walker. A gust of wind blew back her hair, and he was struck by the high, sloping curve of her forehead, the way her hairline started way up in her crown. The effect somehow made her look especially intelligent, which in turn made her all the more attractive balancing there like a girl playing on the rocks in moonlight.

"You're brooding," she said, and climbed down to sit beside him. "It's very romantic."

"I thought I'd let you sleep," he said. "You both fell out like you hadn't slept in days."

"Hadn't," she said. Her blouse was buttoned up to the neck. She grasped her shoulders with her hands, huddled into herself, and shivered. "Jeez," she said. "I remember this little inlet like it was a mountain overlooking the ocean. It's so small."

"I'd offer you my jacket if I had one. You look cold."

"I bet you that sweater's warm," she said.

T started to take off the sweater, and Jenny touched his hand to stop him. "I'm only kidding with you," she said. "Don't take me so seriously."

"Why wouldn't I take you seriously?" He pulled the sweater off and then carefully pushed it over her head and onto her shoulders, holding his hands inside the neck hole and stretching it out so that it would go on easily. When he was close to her, leaning over her, once he had pushed the sweater over the thick profusion of her hair, she tossed her head a little to move the hair away from her eyes and leaned slightly toward him, as if expecting a kiss.

T backed away. He had on a black cotton T. He rubbed his bare arms for warmth.

"Thank you," Jenny said. She touched his chest, laying a hand under his collar bone. "You're really muscled," she said. "You've got to be working out with weights."

"Used to," he said. He looked back toward the line of cabins beyond the inlet. "So what's the story with this place? I peeked in the window. It's nice. Who's Chuck?"

"My uncle," Jenny said. "How'd you know his name?"

"Guy where I got directions. He said he hadn't been here for a while."

"Wouldn't've. Busy man."

"And?" T said. "It would be cruel and unusual not to unravel any of this for me. I mean, I've been a good guy, haven't I? You're not going to make me just drive away without—"

"Why do you have to drive away?" she said. She pouted, dramatically. "Would you leave me here all alone with Lester?"

"I thought that was the deal," he said. "I deliver you, and—"

"But you don't have to," she said. "There's plenty of room." She put her hand on his knee. "You could stay."

"You want me to stay?" T put his hand over hers. "You want me to spend the night here with you and Lester?"

"Yes."

"Why?"

"Because."

"That's not an answer."

"Okay," she said, serious. "Because you have money. Because you have a car. Because we're in trouble, and, honestly—" She hesitated a moment, apparently considering her words. "Maybe you were supposed to pick me up on the side of the road. You sure as hell wouldn't have come into my life any other way."

T said, "You think that you were destined to meet me?"

"Maybe."

T wasn't at all sure what they were talking about anymore. "Let's—" he pressed on. "Let's get some things out of the way."

"Like?"

"Why are you in trouble? What's the life-threatening danger?"

"That's all Lester," she said. "I swear. And it's too long a story for out here." She looked back to the car. "Let's wake up Sleeping Idiot and I'll tell you inside."

"How about a short version?" T said. "Anything. A few clues."

She stood up and offered him a hand. "Lester stole money from people you'd have to be crazy to steal money from— 'axis-of-evil' types. He came to my place and before he was in the house five minutes, the guys he was running from showed up. That was three days ago and we've been hiding and moving ever since."

T took her hand and pulled himself up. "But you—" he said. "You didn't have anything to do with it?"

"Nothing," she said. "I was getting myself back together after a whole bunch of my own trouble. I just bought my house. I was back in school." She suddenly sounded angry. "Don't let's go through the whole thing right now," she said. "There's plenty of time." She started up the rocky incline, leaving T to follow.

At the Rover, T tried to wake Lester, gave up, and then turned his attention to finding a lightweight hooded jacket he knew was somewhere in the vehicle. He found it next to his suitcase and put it on.

Jenny shouted in Lester's ear. "Asshole!" she screamed. "Wake up!"

Lester partially sat up. "All right, all right," he mumbled. "Jesus. Give me a second." Then he lay down again and closed his eyes.

"The hell with him," Jen said. "Let him sleep out here." She slammed the door and started up the hill for the cabin, then turned around after a few steps and came back for her purse in the front seat. "Are you going to stand there looking at him?" she asked T, who had one foot up on the frame in the open back door and was looking down at Lester, trying to decide what to do with him.

T closed the door and stood a moment in the dark watching Jenny as she started again to climb the hill. The red of her pants deepened to wine in the moonlight as she moved with long, angry steps through the black moon shadows of tree branches. His sweater was huge on her and hung loosely from her shoulders. Her pants were molded to her body. A gust of wind off the river ruffled her hair, and she turned around in a pool of moonlight. T was still standing by the Rover, watching her. She looked down at him for several long seconds, her hands on her hips at first, then crossed in front her, watching him watch her.

T hesitated a second longer before he grabbed her backpack, and then went around the car and climbed the hill.

"I must seem like a real bitch to you," she said, turning to continue toward the cabin as he joined her, "the way I'm doing Les."

"Not really, " he said.

She stopped at the top of the hill and looked out over the water. "It's beautiful here. Isn't it?" She gestured to the wide expanse of moonlit river below them.

T stepped in front of her, closer to the ridge, and crouched down, touching the grass with his open hand as he looked below to the Saint Lawrence. "I used to come here as a young man," he said. "When I was in college."

"Where'd you go?" she asked, then crouched alongside him and pointed down the hill. "Is that a boat?"

T didn't see the boat at first but then found it nestled between a pair of rocks, its bow snug against the shore. It was an old V-hull aluminum, fourteen-, maybe sixteen-footer. No oars, no engine. "Looks like it," he said, and he stood and took her arm lightly, continuing toward the cabin.

Jenny leaned into him, as if nuzzling against him for warmth. "So where'd you go to college?" she asked again.

"Syracuse University," T said. He put his arm around her.

"You're sweet," she said.

"I'm counting my blessings," he answered cryptically, not sure himself exactly what he meant.

At the cabin door, Jenny rummaged through her purse, found a key, and struggled with the lock for several seconds before the mechanism finally relented with a dull click. T reached around her, turned the knob, and pushed open the door.

"Shit." She flipped a light switch several times with no effect. "Too much to hope for," she said. She looked back to T. "You bummed?"

"About what? No electricity?" He moved past her into the living room and tossed her backpack onto the cushions of a rustic wood-frame couch, sending up a small mushroom cloud of dust.

"Jesus Christ," Jenny said, closing the door. "The place is filthy. And it's cold."

"It's not bad," he said. "Why don't you see if there's blankets and bedding?" He went into the kitchen and tried the sink. "We've got running water," he called as Jenny disappeared down the hallway.

"Plenty of bedding," her voice came back to him. Then she appeared in the kitchen doorway holding an armful of blankets and sheets. "Will you stay?"

"Sure. Why not?" He turned the kitchen faucet on and off. "No hot water, though."

"Damn. I was looking forward to—" She looked at the counter. "Is that from mice?" she asked.

"Afraid so."

"God," she said. "I hate mice. I know it's girly, but—You don't think there's rats?"

"Just field mice, I'm sure," T said. "They get in during winter."

Jenny looked suddenly and deeply unhappy.

"Go make the beds," T said. "I'll clean up in here." He knelt and opened the cabinets under the sink. "Look at this." He pulled out a blue plastic pail overflowing with cleaning supplies. "We're in business."

Jenny watched him quietly as he went about dampening a rag and wiping off the counters. She stood in the doorway piled down with bedding. "You don't have to do that," she said.

He pushed the mouse droppings off the countertop and into the trash pail he had found under the sink. "I don't mind," he said, and then stopped when he realized she was standing with her arms full of bedding observing him as if amazed by his behavior and slightly wary, as if she were watching a large foreign animal in the kitchen and wasn't at all sure it might not turn on her. He tried to reassure her. "I wasn't going any-place," he said. "I'm having fun here." He pointed toward the bedrooms. "Go. Go make the beds."

While she was busy in the bedrooms, T finished wiping down the counters and then dusted the furniture. He took the couch and chair cushions outside to bang them into each other and slap them with the handle of a broom he had found in the otherwise empty kitchen pantry, and then he went about sweeping the dusty floors. He liked cleaning. Something about the mindless, repetitive swirl of activity calmed him. Mornings, while the coffee brewed, he liked to wash the few plates and cups from the prior evening's snacking. He liked the feel of warm water running over his hands while he turned a ceramic cup or plate, going over it with a soft, soapy sponge. He enjoyed doing things with an empty head, and cleaning was the right activity for that, requiring just enough attention to pass the time outside himself. And then, when he was done, there were results. Things were clean, and neat, and in order.

In Salem, his house was immaculate. Day after day living there he had cleaned and recleaned and cleaned again. More than once he had found himself standing at the kitchen table with a dish rag in hand while he stared out the window at nothing but sky and the bulk of his thickly treed mountain, the one that rose up in the near distance and hovered endlessly unmoving over his house. His time in Salem had required him to tap a lifetime of resources. He philosophized. He told himself to live in the moment, to accept whatever it gave, to immerse himself in the experience. He tried to see things truly. He argued to himself that seeing things clearly and truly and acknowledging his situation would be the first step before he could figure out what to do next and how to move on. He was sure he would eventually move on, that his life would start up again, that it was only a matter of time. He read novels, classic and modern. He read poetry, mostly modern and contemporary. He listened to jazz almost constantly. He exercised. He was not the kind of man who was meant to live alone. Isolation was an agony to be endured, and he did pull-ups and push-ups and leg lifts. He bought a free standing gym and used it daily. He power-walked at least two miles every day, often several times that. He drank one to two glasses of wine a day, traveling north to Roanoke or south to Blacksburg to buy the best vintages. He played computer games: Myst and Doom and a dozen others, chess on the Internet, all the sports games on PlayStation 2. More than once he'd found himself at two or three in the morning working the controls of a computer game when his engagement in the virtual action suddenly ceased of its own accord and he saw himself, a man in his fifties up in the middle of the night, alone, totally engaged in an utterly meaningless virtual world, and each time it happened, he felt ashamed. And he felt something very close to shock. How did he get to such a place? How did it happen? He cleaned; he listened to jazz; he played computer games; he exercised; he collected and consumed wine; in time he got into photography, buying equipment, taking pictures, trying to learn PhotoShop; and one by one the months passed until there was more than a year's worth of them and if anything essential had changed he didn't know what. He was pushing his way through time like a swimmer working to cross a huge body of water.

"We can make a fire," Jenny said. She came out of one of the bedrooms with a white quilt wrapped around her shoulders like a cape. "There's a great fireplace in the bedroom."

"Did you check the flue?" T asked.

"That's better," she said, noticing the countertops in the kitchen. She went to the window, which looked out over the river. "I love the views here."

"It's a great cabin." T joined her in the kitchen. "What's your uncle do?"

"CPA," she said. "But we don't want to talk about Uncle Chuck." She leaned against the window and watched him a moment. "You're handsome," she said. "You look good in moonlight."

"Think so? Moonlight hide my age?"

"You're old," she pronounced, as if she had been considering the subject, "but you're sexy too. You're one of those sexy older guys it's easy to get off on, like Richard Gere, kind of; or, no, Sean Connery. Who wouldn't want to get down with Sean Connery? You're kind of like that," she said. "I bet you know it, too."

"You're flattering me."

"I'm not," she said. She looked down at her legs as if remembering something and then rubbed them briskly with the palms of her hands. "I've got to get out of these things," she said. "Ever worn leather several days straight?" When T didn't answer, she added, "I didn't think so. How about this for a plan? You make a fire. Meanwhile, I get out of these pants and take a quick, cold shower. Then, when I'm done, I can warm up with you in front of the flames."

"Did you check the flue?" T asked again.

She shook her head. "Think it's a problem?"

"I've got a flashlight in the Rover," he said. "You go ahead. It'll probably be fine."

She wrapped her arms around him and planted a loud kiss on his cheek. "There's wood in the thingamajig by the fireplace." She grabbed her backpack from the couch, clutched it to her chest, and disappeared into the back of the cabin.

Outside, there was a definite chill in the air. It felt like a storm might be coming on. T hugged himself and put the hood up on his jacket. He hurried through the shadows to the Rover, where he found Lester in exactly the same position, with his nose in the seam between the seat cushion and back-rest. When he saw the bucket of fried chicken on the floor, he realized he was hungry. He opened the container and was amused to find half the chicken gone. He wouldn't have thought she could eat that much, and he wondered if perhaps Lester had pulled himself up out of sleep long enough to eat a fried-chicken dinner. He imagined them both munching on cold fried chicken, wondering where the old guy had gone off to, and then Lester going back to sleep while Jenny went out to look around. Or she might just be a small girl with a big appetite. He grabbed a chicken leg from the bucket, took the Mag light from the glove compartment, and went around to the back of the Rover for his suitcase. After he finished off the drumstick and before he closed the hatchback, he remembered the emergency supplies stored near the spare tire and retrieved a blanket-sized fleece tightly rolled and packed into a clear plastic container. He pushed the guitar case aside and crawled to the back seat, where he spread the fleece over Lester.

After lugging his oversized suitcase up the hill and laying it on the bed, he checked the flue, shining the flashlight beam up the chimney shaft. Not seeing anything worrisome—blockages of leaves, bird nests, thick incrustations of creosote—he piled three logs on top of several small pieces of kindling and pulled down a round container of matches from the mantel. To get the fire started, he retrieved the current *New Yorker* from his suitcase, tore out a dozen glossy pages, crumpling them into crushed balls of print, and wedged them under the soot-charred andirons. A few minutes later the fire was crackling, the first flames taking hold in the kindling as smoke pooled worrisomely for a moment before being drawn up the flue.

From the bathroom came the sound of a running shower. Water splashed so loud and distinct against porcelain, he could almost see the blocked flow, the fat, twisting stream in the center where minerals had caked the small, concentric circles of tiny holes. He guessed the bathroom door wasn't completely closed, and when he went quietly out into the hall, his guess was confirmed. The door was ajar the width of a man's fist. The red light of the fire, now crackling and snapping, lit up the hallway where he stood. He backed out of the light into a second, smaller bedroom and saw, in the dark, that the bed had not been made, though a fat comforter and what looked like a pillow and sheets were stacked neatly at the foot of the mattress. He went out into the hallway again and slid along the wall into a tongue of shadow, where he saw Jenny's reflection in a sliver of mirror. She was undressed with her back turned to him, in the process of pulling her hair behind her head and fastening it somehow. She looked to be tying it back, as if with a ribbon or a rubber band. Her arms were raised and he could see the sides of her breasts, full and weighty in muted moonlight coming from a window behind the drawn shower curtain. Half of her back was draped in shadow so that the undulating course of her spine seemed to divide her between light and dark. She had no tattoos. He thought every young woman these days was tattooed. As far as he could see, she had no moles or scars to mar the lines of her body. When she dropped her arms, having finished tying back her hair, he moved away quietly, fearing she might turn and see his reflection in the mirror watching her.

He took off his jacket and lay down in front of the fire on the bearskin rug, looking absently a moment at the mounted head in profile: the dog-like ears, the snout and white teeth that looked sharp enough still to be dangerous. He ran his fingers though the fur and asked himself what he would do if, as appeared to be a distinct possibility, Jenny was planning to sleep with him. He hadn't had sex in more than two years. His entire sex life these past two years had consisted of occasional, boredom-induced masturbation. He seemed to have lost the ability to successfully fantasize. In his youth, his fantasies were wild. He dreamed of sex with multiple women, a woman on his back with him atop a woman on her back; sex with couples; sex with dozens; massive orgies. Fantasy after fantasy brought him to crackling orgasm. In his youth. When he woke up every morning of his life with a raging erection. Which had stopped exactly when? At forty? Forty-five? Now he woke with only the need to pee. Now his old fantasies all struck him as ridiculous and shallow. Whereas in his youth the women all moaned with pleasure as he pounded himself to orgasm, now they tended to evaporate within minutes of their conjuring, leaving him holding his halfhearted member in hand as he drifted off to sleep. Now, after seeing Jenny naked in the shower—a beautiful young woman who was apparently interested in him—he found himself more worried about actually having sex with her than looking forward to it.

He conjured again the image of Jenny in moonlight tying up her hair, but the picture faded after a moment or two, and then he was thinking about the cover of a slim book of contemporary poetry he had purchased recently. It was a reproduction of Thomas Hart Benton's *Persephone*. Snuggled in the hollows of a gnarled oak tree, unclothed Persephone's perfect body radiates the splendid luxury of youth, while behind her an old man with thin gray hair and features twisted into ugliness by age reaches one arthritic hand toward her thigh. T pushed the image out of mind. He wasn't old and arthritic. He hadn't crept away from his horse-drawn cart to spy on innocent Persephone. He had picked up Jenny and her companion hitchhiking. He had delivered them where they wanted to go. At Jenny's request, at her urging, he had agreed to spend the night in her uncle's cabin. As for the old man's lust in the

Benton painting, about that he didn't know. He wasn't sure what he was doing. He didn't know what he wanted. All he knew for absolute certain was that he preferred being where he was, in front of a fire in a cabin on the Thousand Islands waiting for Jenny to take her shower, to where he had previously been headed, which would most likely have been a generic, sanitized motel room separated by four walls from everyone else in the world.

The sound of the shower curtain being pulled aside in the bathroom bounced out into the empty hallway, followed in a moment by Jenny's inarticulate squeals and articulate curses—*Oh, shit; motherfucker; son of a bitch*—and the interrupted rhythms of water splashing off a body and onto porcelain. Then the water stopped, the curtain was pulled back, and the sound of scurrying feet preceded her appearance in the bedroom doorway wrapped in a blue towel held together by one fist at her breasts, but not long enough to cover her. She stood a moment shivering in the doorway. After the first instant's reflexive dropping of his eyes, T fixed his gaze on her face.

"Water a little cold?" he asked.

"Think so?" she said, and dropped the towel as she pulled the white quilt off the bed, threw it over her shoulders, and lay down on the rugs in front of T by the fire. She pulled the quilt tightly around her, tucking the edges under her thighs and legs, and pushed her body back into T. "Put your arms around me," she said, turning to look into his face, "before I freeze to death." She kissed him on the cheek.

T put his arms around her. Her head rested on his bicep as he held her tight.

"Ummm," she purred. "This is delicious." She snuggled into him, molding her body to the contours of his and closing her eyes drowsily.

T touched her bare shoulder with his cheek, and she turned in his arms onto her back and kissed him on the lips, her hand under the quilt pushing up under his T shirt and along his ribs to his chest.

T knew what was supposed to happen next. This was the moment when he kissed her in return and then fumbled out of his clothes as he raised himself up over her and onto her and then pushed himself into her for the familiar warm rocking and thrust and moan of sex, but instead of the rising and filling and swell the moment required, he felt come over him a sense of deflation, as if his body from head to toe were going so soft it might liquefy. What he felt was sadness flowing through him, deep sadness. He leaned away from her under the quilt, making enough distance to look her in the eyes. "I don't know what I'm doing here," he said.

Jenny seemed puzzled. She leaned back on her elbow and propped her head up on her hand. "What do you mean?" she asked. "What do you mean, you don't know what you're doing?"

"I don't," T said. "I just— Why? Why would you—"

"Why's a dumb question." She touched his lips with her finger. "I want you to make love to me. I just want you to."

T watched her watching him, her eyes on his eyes, and knew she was expecting him to start again, to lean into her with the kiss that would put the act in motion. He didn't. He waited.

"You picked us up," she said. She sounded bewildered. "You brought us here. You cleaned up the cabin while I made the beds. You built a fire while I took a shower. Plus, I see the way you look at me. What did you think we were doing? What did you think was happening?"

T watched the fire, where the flames were shooting up from the kindling through charred gaps in the big logs. Already a bed of red embers pulsed beneath the andirons. "Jenny," he said, and heard his voice as a dramatic harsh whisper. He coughed and tried again. "Apparently I'm not—" he said. He kissed her shoulder through the quilt. "This is sweet, though, holding you like this."

"Oh my God," she said, and she touched the back of his neck. "You're so— You don't want to make love to me?" She stroked the back of his head. "Is there something— Are you afraid I might have AIDS, or—"

"No," T said. "That's not—"

"Because I have condoms."

"Jenny," T said. "It's not about—"

"I don't have any diseases, Aloysius. Mr. Walker. I'm not a whore."

"I don't think you're a whore."

"Oh, please. Why wouldn't—" She stopped and rubbed

his back gently. "Listen," she said, "don't lie to me. You must think I'm a whore. Why wouldn't you think that?"

"I don't think like that," he said finally. "I just, don't—"

"Well, I do," she said. "And now— You turn out— Oh, Jesus Christ."

T looked up from the fire and saw that her face was wet. "Jenny," he said, and wiped a tear away from her eye with a corner of the quilt.

"I feel humiliated."

"Because I didn't—"

"Because I've been acting like a whore," she said, articulating each word, insisting on it. "Let's not bullshit, please. And then you turn out to actually be decent."

"I'm not decent," T said quickly. "I swear. No one thinks I'm decent."

"Well, you are," she said. "And how could you not think of me as anything but some pathetic little tramp?"

"Jenny—"

"At least let me explain." She sat up, wrapped herself tightly in the quilt, and slid away from T, toward the fire. She crossed her legs under her.

Out from under the quilt, T felt as though he were the one who was naked. He experienced the loss of her warmth like a shock and actually shivered as he looked around for something with which to cover himself. He found his jacket near the foot of the bed.

"I've been acting like a little slut from the moment we

met," she said. She spoke with the quilt wrapped around her. "For God's sake, I just came in here naked and threw myself on you."

"You didn't throw yourself—"

"Yes, I did. It's humiliating. But, please— You have to understand what Lester's done. It's just— It's unbelievable, T."

"All right," he said. "But I swear I'm not thinking of you as a whore or a slut or any such thing."

"Of course you are!" she said, and a little bubble of mucus blew up and popped under her nose. "Oh, Christ—" She pointed with her chin to where her drawstring purse lay near the bed. "Could you get me a tissue?"

T handed her the purse.

She blew her nose and threw the tissue into the fire, where it was eaten up immediately in a bright yellow flame. "I've been behaving like a tramp," she said, composed. "At least let me have the dignity of admitting it. I have been, but you have to understand, I'm terrified. I'm frightened for my life." With those words, the tears came again. She seemed to give up on wiping them away. "I've been behaving badly, but my life is threatened. Lester stole money from a guy who everybody knows is a sick, murdering, torturing perv. We spent the last two nights hiding in my wine cellar, terrified, while this guy and the sick biker assholes who work for him totally destroyed my house."

"What? Like the Wild Bunch?"

"The what?"

"Never mind," T said, realizing she probably wouldn't even know Marlon Brando let alone the Wild Bunch. "I'm having a hard time visualizing this," he said. "Where was your house? What do you mean bikers destroyed it?"

"It was my mother's house first," she said, and pulled the quilt tighter around her. "I had just bought it in September; I had just finally gotten the money together . . ." She stopped a moment and shook her head, as if to compose herself and keep from crying yet again. "It's outside of Chattanooga. It's a small house, but it's on five acres, which is why it was so hard to raise the money. It used to be a plantation a gazillion years ago. This is going back to the Civil War."

"You own a house on five acres of land?"

"Wrecked house," she said. "They tore it apart so bad it'll have to be rebuilt."

"Because of Lester?"

"They couldn't figure out where the hell we were." She paused and took a breath, as if gathering her thoughts, then gave him a look that announced she was about to tell the story, and he should just relax and listen. "Lester," she said, starting off slowly. "Lester, who's never had an entrepreneurial notion in his life, hatches this plan to steal money from these monsters and then he's going to buy coke and resell it and replace the money, and nobody's ever going to know about it. Of course he gets ripped off, and when it dawns on him that he's now a dead man, he comes to my house looking to borrow money so he can run to Canada."

"This is a few days ago," T said.

"Three days ago now," she answered. "He's not there two minutes, at my house— I mean, he just came in the door, a half-dozen bikes and cars come screaming down the drive. I have no idea what's going on yet, but Lester's panicked, so I hide him, us, in the wine cellar, which goes back to Prohibition. It's hidden under a trapdoor under a fake boiler. They never found it, but they tore the house down looking for us. They're like, *We know they're in here. We saw them go in; we didn't see them go out.* We can hear it all from the wine cellar, where we're curled up like a couple of rats, scared to death. Eventually they decided we slipped out somehow. After they left, we gathered a few things and ran. We hitched a ride with a trucker into Virginia, and then a perv insurance salesman who couldn't keep his hands off me took us to Tully, where we spent the last of the money we had between us on breakfast. Then we stood there by the side of the road all day until you picked us up."

When she finished her story, T looked away from her, into the fire, at the growing bed of embers, its pulsing red surface crisscrossed with crackling white rivers of heat. He wondered if she would ask him for the money they needed to get straight with the bad guys outright at this point, or if she'd wait for him to offer it. And if he offered right now, he wondered if she'd decline and wait for him to offer again in the morning, to offer perhaps several times, until he was practically begging her to let him help, and then, only then, finally, taking the money reluctantly. He looked into the embers and considered how much he could give her. He knew he'd give her something. He just didn't know how much yet.

"Oh my God," she said, and she touched her mouth with two fingers, as if she might blow him a kiss. "Oh my God," she repeated. "You don't believe me. You don't believe any of it."

T was surprised and embarrassed. He lied immediately. "No. Of course I believe you," he said.

Her face seemed to collapse, as if a huge tiredness had overcome her. She lay down in front of the fire and curled up inside the quilt. "All right," she said. "I need to get some sleep."

T watched her as she closed her eyes and laid her cheek on the balled-up fabric of the quilt. Above her head, one of the bear's dog-like ears stood up as if listening for what would happen next. The fire crackled and filled the room with the smell of wood smoke. He touched her shoulder and she opened her eyes to look up at him. He had the urge to tell her how beautiful she was. "Jenny," he said. "I believe you."

She nodded, acknowledging his effort at kindness and at the same time signaling it had no effect. "You know what I'd like?" she whispered, her voice so drained even the volume was gone. "It was nice when you were holding me. Could you just do that for me, please? Could you just hold me till I fall asleep?"

T gathered the pillows from the bed and crawled under the quilt with her, holding her as he had before, his arms around her, her head on his bicep, but with a pillow now between her head and his skin. She closed her eyes and then opened them again to watch the fire a while in silence, then closed them again. Tears seeped out from under her eyelashes, not drops, just a flow, a thick wetness seeping out, spreading to her cheek, pooling between her eye and the bridge of her nose. With a corner of his pillowcase he wiped the tears away, but said nothing and she said nothing.

He supposed her story could be true, the whole implausible thing. He doubted it, but, really, he didn't care. He looked down at the young woman wrapped up with him in a quilt and watched her a while with the palpable sense of holding a mystery in his arms. She twisted around, making herself comfortable, snuggling against his chest, and he saw that she was close to sleep, and then he put his own head down on a pillow on the bear's head, and closed his eyes, and drifted toward darkness thinking of her as a foreign creature in bed with him, her breath against his chest, amazed—though it was a lesson he had already learned well—amazed still at how rapidly at least the outward circumstances of a life could change.

He woke to Jenny nuzzling blindly into him for warmth, throwing a leg over his thigh and seemingly attempting to glue the front of her body to the front of his. It took him a second to remember where he was. He had no idea of the time, only that the temperature had dropped significantly and the wind had picked up outside. He could hear a loud soughing in the trees. It felt late. It felt like the deepest hours of the night. In the moonlight through the window on the other side of the room, smoke drifted near the ceiling and moved from side to side with each loud gust of wind. The fire had burned down to quiet embers, and the fiercest gusts of wind were pushing smoke down the flue and into the bedroom. He seemed to remember from fireplaces in the past that this was not a big problem. Still, he thought he should probably open a window an inch or so, and he lifted himself up on one elbow, peeling away from Jenny, who then folded up her body like a child, pulling her knees toward her chest, clamping her legs around her clasped hands, and burrowing down into the layers of rugs.

In the process of extricating himself from the tangled quilt, he caught a glimpse of Jenny's body, her breasts framed between her arms, the tight flesh of her stomach, the triangle of her sex where her hands were pushed between her legs. She had shaved herself there in a narrow strip, which he had noticed before, when she had first come into the bedroom from the shower. He had wondered then, as he did again at this moment, why she would shave like that, given it wasn't the time of year for bikinis. While contemplating her body, he was immensely pleased to feel his own body responding. He unbuttoned his jeans and looked down at a hard and arching erection with a feeling not unlike the pleasure of running unexpectedly into an old friend. It had been a very long time since he had experienced this degree of youthful readiness for sex, and for a moment he seriously considered initiating the act while she was still sleeping, remembering how Brooke had once told him there was nothing she loved better than waking up being fucked. He touched Jenny's thigh lightly, but as soon as the thought of sex moved out of the realm of the hypothetical and toward the realm of the actual, a voice in the back of his head laughed at him and asked what the hell he thought he was doing. This girl was twenty-three, younger than his own daughter. Considerably younger. Did he believe for one second that she could be genuinely attracted to him? No, he didn't. With that acknowledgment, his old friend waved good-bye and disappeared. T buttoned up, tucked the quilt around Jenny, and got up to open a window.

Outside, the trees were trembling in a steady wind, and the river seethed under lines of white foam. He opened the window an inch and then stood a long time with his arms crossed on the windowsill looking out at the night. He tried hard to concentrate on the physical world, the world of trees and rocks, of wind and water. He tried to feel himself as a creature alive in the physical world, an animate being in the phenomenal world, someone to whom anything might happen and capable of setting into effect an infinite sequence of actions. Tom Walker, a human being alive for a stunningly brief span of years on a small planet circling a medium-sized star in an unimaginably massive universe. He tried hard to feel the gift of being alive right then at that moment—and he did. He felt it and was grateful, and was able to hold on to the feeling for a second or two before his thoughts shifted to Alicia, his most recent ex, whom he had met some twenty-four years ago when she was almost exactly the same age as the young woman currently sleeping in front of the fire across the room from him. Moving from one mode of perception to the other, from the metaphysical to the personal, was like walking out of a beautiful countryside and into a prison, and yet he couldn't help himself. He stared out a cabin window at the Saint Lawrence River on a windy and extraordinary night and thought his pedestrian thoughts about his own life.

He had met Alicia a little more than a year after Brooke left him. He had an apartment downtown, just outside the old meat-packing district, with a view of the Hudson, and with the help of some friends he knew through Brooke, he had invested enough money in an Off-Broadway play to earn a producer listing, which in turn earned him the right to quietly observe rehearsals. He was still in his early thirties then, and hardly wealthy, but his various businesses were doing well, and to Alicia, he realized, he must have appeared to be rich. She was twenty-two, a little more than a year out of SUNY Purchase, with a BFA, an eight-month-old son, and no child support from the father, who was still in college. She lived with her parents in Massapequa, Long Island, and commuted into the city to work days in a coffee shop and nights on the play while leaving her son, Evan, to be raised by his grandparents. She was a tall woman, taller than T when she wore her hair up, and she had a dancer's body, muscular and lithe. It wasn't lost on T that physically she was Brooke's opposite. The contrast with Brooke was striking in every way. Where Brooke was flighty and unstable, Alicia was focused and resolute. Where Brooke never seemed to know what she wanted or even why she should want anything, which T attributed to her coming from a wealthy family and inheriting wealth, Alicia was superb at focusing on a goal and doing whatever needed to be done to achieve it. When T met her, she was working eight-hour shifts at the coffee shop, grabbing a quick bite to eat and then taking the subway downtown, where she would rehearse all night, sometimes into the early hours of the morning, before catching a ride home with the director, who also lived out on the island. Once T got to know her a little, he started giving her rides home, and they quickly discovered the similarity of their circumstances. T was still principally living in Huntington, Long Island, and raising his six-year-old daughter, Maura, alone, with the help of his mother, who was only too glad to get involved since her husband, T's father, had died suddenly a few years earlier. By opening night, T and Alicia were spending a couple of evenings a week together alone in his apartment, and most weekends together with the kids, eight-month-old Evan and six-year old Maura. By the time the play closed six months later, a qualified Off-Broadway success, they were married.

And thus. That was the way his life flowed.

Alicia, Evan, Maura, and T. For many, many years.

Maura grew up and married and moved away.

Evan grew up and went off to college.

T worked hard. T made money. T grew more and more isolated in his work. He worked, and he worked, and he worked more. The money grew and grew.

Alicia grew up too, and somewhere along the line, without T noticing, stopped loving him. In time she fell in love with someone else. Another actor. Several years younger. They must have fallen deeply in love. T had no clue. Not until long after his exile to Salem. Not until the papers were all signed and the documents certified and Alicia owned most of what they had previously both owned. Then he found out.

Looking out the window at the Saint Lawrence, T's thoughts skittered away from the day Alicia had driven down to Virginia to explain to him, furious and through tears, why he was responsible for all that had transpired, and then lingered on the early years, when her son, Evan, loved him as a father and his daughter, Maura, loved Alicia, if not completely as a mother, since Brooke was still in the picture, then at least as someone terribly important to her, someone she trusted and depended upon. He recalled those many years when the kids were still kids. He remembered the vacations they had taken together, to Greece and Italy, to the Scandinavian countries; he thought of the fjords and the Alps and the Mediterranean. He remembered, in particular, a summery night on Sea Island, off the coast of Georgia, during an August two-week family vacation, walking along the beach at night barefoot and hand in hand with Alicia while Evan ran in and out of the waves and Maura stuck close to Evan, looking after him; and for some reason he remembered the bicycles. Bicycling along the beach was one of the principal vacation activities there, and a bicycle or a group of bicycles would appear regularly in the moonlight, preceded by the sticky sound of tires spinning up sand. It was not a walk during which anything dramatic happened. It was not the night the four of them came across an alligator in the surf and called the Forest Service, and then watched as the creature was captured and hauled away in the back of an SUV. It was an uneventful night: just the four of them on a moonlight walk along a white-sand beach with bicyclists. He held Alicia's hand. Both the children called him "Daddy." Evan running back to him with a shell or some sea dreck saying, "Daddy? What's this?" Maura complaining, "Daddy. Evan's going in up to his knees!" How small they were then. How different the world.

Behind him, Jenny made a soft, whimpering sound. She was wrapped up in a little ball, so near to the dead fire she was in danger of going up in flames should the quilt get pushed any closer to the embers. He picked her up easily, a hand under her shoulder and the other under her knees, placed her down gently on the bed, and then covered her with two thick green blankets, which he found on a shelf in the room's only closet. From the wood carrier he took the last two split logs and placed them over the embers on the andiron. He used more of his *New Yorker* to get the fire going, then backed away from the hearth toward the middle of the room and took a second to look over the scene: Jenny asleep in a sleigh bed under a pile of blankets in the flickering firelight; the constant hum of the wind around the house and through the trees and over the water; the regular loud gusts of wind beginning as a soft moan and building to screams; the little cloud of smoke, thinner now but still there, hovering near the ceiling; the smell of wood smoke; the chill of cold air against his bare arms; the shadows; the moonlight through the window.

He considered leaving. It seemed like a good moment to simply walk out of this story. Jenny and Lester go on with their lives. T goes on with his. Instead, he went to the kitchen for a drink of water, the fireplace heat and smoke having parched his throat, and found Lester sitting on the counter by the kitchen window huddled up inside one of the same deep-green blankets he had just put over Jenny. His back was against the wall, his knees were pulled to his chest, and he looked out the window and down to the water as if he hadn't heard T walk into the kitchen, or the small gasp T made when he first saw the figure of a man wrapped in a blanket sitting on a kitchen counter.

T said, "How long have you been here?"

Lester didn't acknowledge his presence. He stared out the window to the river in silence.

T poured himself a glass of water from the kitchen sink and nearly choked on the first mouthful, which tasted thick with sulfur. He held the water glass under his nose and then jerked his head back from the unpalatable odor.

"So," Lester said, looking at T for the first time, "how was it?"

"Water's terrible," he said. He put the glass down, leaned back against the sink facing Lester, and grasped the counter-top with the palms of his hands. "How was what?"

"Jenny," Lester said. "Sleeping with Jenny. How was it?"

T met Lester's eyes, which were narrow and glaring, and returned his hard gaze with one sleepy and comfortable.

Lester turned back to the window. "She doesn't like it, you know."

"Doesn't like what?"

"Sex," he said. "She doesn't like sex."

"She doesn't? Ever? With anyone?"

"She'd rather get a tooth pulled. Why? Did she do the whole act for you? Did she have an earthshaking orgasm?" Lester looked as though he were crouched inside his blanket, as if, should he want to, he could leap from the counter. "She did, didn't she?" he said, settling the matter. He touched his head back against the wall and looked up, in the direction of the moon. "Forget it," he added. "It was an act. It hurts her, physically. Her vagina actually physically hurts when she has sex."

"She told you that?" T said. "What? Always? It's always hurt her to have sex?"

Lester said, "You think you know something about Jenny?" He shook his head, as if despairing of T's ignorance.

"I don't think I know anything about Jenny." T took a step toward Lester and then stood there awkwardly in the middle of the kitchen.

"Fuck," Lester said, as if too disgusted to continue the conversation. He covered his face with his hands. "I'm tired."

T watched him a moment longer, then started aimlessly out of the kitchen toward the living room before noticing the guitar case propped up against the wall. He touched the hard plastic shell, running his fingers over one of the metal snaps. "Are you a musician?" he asked.

Lester shook his head.

"What's in the guitar case?"

"Red guitar." He took his hands away from his face. "It's valuable." He turned his back to the window and slid his legs off the counter. "I'll sleep on the couch," he said, and then paused a moment, thoughtfully. "I just wanted you to know about Jenny. I'm not bullshitting you. I lived with her for a year. I watched her go through all her stuff."

"All what stuff?"

Lester pulled the blanket around him and hunched his shoulders as if he were cold. "Just— I know a little bit about her," he said. "It hurts her to have sex. It's one of the reasons we split up. I mean, she'd do it, for me, but I was like—" He slid down from the counter. "I just thought you should know."

T said, "I didn't have sex with Jenny."

"Please." Lester tugged at his blanket. "I got this out of your closet. I walked right past you."

"I didn't have sex with her," T repeated, and went out into the hallway. He ignored the questioning look on Lester's face. "I'll sleep in the back bedroom," he said. "There's another bedroom across from the bathroom, if you don't want to sleep on the couch."

Lester picked up the guitar case. "I don't mind couches. Spent half my life sleeping on couches."

T looked past him out the kitchen window. The moon had moved out of sight, but he could still see its light reflecting on the river. "Well . . ." he said, and he started down the hallway. Behind him, he heard Lester take a few steps out of the kitchen, and when he turned around to close the bedroom door, he saw him standing in the hallway, looking back at him, a long-haired young man draped in a green blanket, holding what he claimed was a red guitar.

He stood silently a while in the dark with his ear close to the door, and after the house was silent for several minutes, the only sounds the wind and an occasional loud pop from the burning logs, he undressed in the dark down to his underwear and undershirt, laid his clothes on top of the room's single dresser, and climbed into bed under a weighty comforter and yet another of the plentiful green blankets. He lay on his back, bent the pillow in half to prop his head up higher, and folded his hands over his chest. He was tired, and he could tell it wouldn't take him long to fall asleep. He let his thoughts slip back to Jenny fixing her hair in the moonlit bathroom, and then to Jenny again as she came through the bedroom door holding a towel around her, and then the moment when she let the towel drop before settling under the quilt with him. He tried to hold those moments in his mind's eye for as long as he could, until he felt himself sinking toward sleep with the image of Jenny's body floating over him, the flawless lines and curves of her torso and belly, the perfect weight of her breasts, and as he was imagining her, remaking her image out of memory and desire, the real Jenny pushed open the bedroom door trailing the white quilt over her shoulder and stood there panicky for a moment. "T?" she said. "T? Where are you?"

T sat up in bed, shaking off sleep, and before he could say a word Jenny hurried under the covers with him. She was sobbing. Her face was so wet with tears that his undershirt soaked through as soon as she laid her head upon his chest. "Don't leave me like that," she whispered, and he felt her whole body shake with sobs and quiver like a child's with quick, convulsive gasps.

He put an arm around her back. He smoothed her hair. "How long have you been crying?" he asked.

Between sobs, she answered, "I cry at night sometimes," and then, "I wake up crying." She pressed her body against his so hard and insistent it was as if she were trying to crawl inside him.

"It's okay," he said. He held the back of her head in the palm of his hand. "It's okay," he repeated, and he felt her body loosen slightly in his arms while her sobs diminished, slowly changing to deep and rhythmic breathing as she bit by bit relaxed in his arms.

T awoke to the low rumble of thunder and the patter of rain against the bedroom window. He opened his eyes to morning light that seeped into the room through dusty, rose-colored blinds, giving the floorboards and single dresser and narrow bed a somber, rose-tinged aura. Alongside him, Jenny slept peacefully on her side, facing the closed bedroom door with the comforter pulled up to her neck so that all T could see of her was a bright blond profusion of hair spilling over the pillow and the shape of her body curled in an S under the quilt. He folded his pillow to prop up his head, lay on his back with his hands clasped over his chest, and watched the play of light on the ceiling for a minute before he decided to drive into town for supplies and then come back and make breakfast.

He carried his clothes into the master bedroom, where he sat on the still warm rugs in front of the dead fire and dressed. The cabin was quieter even than his home in Virginia, which he had thought, after living a lifetime in New York, was the quietest place on earth. Here, though, the only sound was the rain. If there were boats on the Saint Lawrence, they were either moving silently or they were too far away to hear. No cars. No airplanes. No people. Not even the hum of a refrigerator or the drone of a heating system. Not even, this morning, any wind. Only the soft tapping of a light rain as he pulled on his shoes and slipped into his jacket before creeping down the hall to the living room, where he had expected to find Lester asleep on the couch. Instead of Lester, he saw his photography equipment—a pair of tripods, two leather camera bags, and another equipment bag—in the center of the room atop a crumpled green blanket, as if Lester, after removing the equipment from the Rover, had taken care not to damage anything by laying it directly on the floor.

Outside, the grass that grew up to the concrete foundation was slick and wet. He needed to walk only a few feet for an unobstructed view down the hill to the big oak where he had parked the Rover, and where, as he would have guessed, it was no longer parked. From the tire tracks in the mud, he could see where it had been backed up and turned around toward the blacktop. On the road itself, the muddy tire tracks started thick and then faded in the direction of Alexandria Bay. When he remembered that he had left the car keys in his pants pocket, he reached for his wallet, which, of course, wasn't there either.

He closed his eyes and lowered his head and waited in the rain for the first rush of anger and frustration to pass. The sky was a mass of fat clouds moving slowly out to the sea. In daylight, the isolation and the beauty of the area were evident. In front of him, the single road that twisted along the bottom of the hill bracketed by green expanses of trees was the only sign of commerce. Behind him, the row of empty cabins and the river.

He wiped rain away from his eyes and went around to the back of the cabin, where he found a boulder against a tree and sat with his arms crossed and his knees up, huddled into himself, watching the river, which seemed to be moving rapidly, or at least that was the illusion it gave looking down on it from his height, at his angle. Water smacked the rocks on the shore as white streaks of foam appeared and disappeared all the way across to the Canadian side, only a few miles distant. Scattered across the river were scores of tiny islands interwoven with narrow waterways. T watched the river roll past in the rain for a minute or two, then rose to his feet without premeditation, as if some invisible puppeteer decided to work his strings. He started back for the bedroom, where Jenny was most likely still sleeping. He was soaked. And cold. He could almost feel the warmth of her sleeping body snuggled under covers.

He found her, however, already awake. She lay on her side just as he had left her, only now her eyes were open. They followed him as he walked down the hall.

"You're all wet," she said.

T stood in the doorway dripping water. "Lester took the Rover and my wallet. He's gone."

"Probably went to town to get food," she said. "He took the whole wallet?"

"Took the keys and wallet out of my pants, while we were sleeping."

"He's so paranoid," she said. "He probably just wanted to make sure we didn't go anyplace without him."

"You think he's coming back?"

Jenny smiled as if his misperceptions were too cute for words. She stretched her feet under the covers. "Trust me," she said. "He'll be back."

T watched her for a moment while she stared back at him in amusement. She looked cozy buried under the covers, only her head peeking out above the quilt. He considered asking her how she could be so sure Lester would be back, but decided against it. Instead, he went into the bathroom and peeled off his wet clothes.

"How'd you get so wet?" she called to him.

"Sitting on a rock watching the river."

"That's so romantic."

He sat down on the john and struggled out of his pants. "Where'd Lester think we'd go without a car?"

"Lester's weird," she said. "Who knows?"

"Any idea why he'd take my photography equipment out of the Rover and bring it in here?"

She was silent a moment, and he imagined her in the next room curled up comfortably inside her little cocoon, the way her eyes might be gazing intently at nothing as she gathered her thoughts. He was surprised at how vividly her image had lodged itself in his mind, especially her eyes, which he felt he still had not been able to read accurately, and so the image of them, green and gazing at something intently, was a kind of puzzle, an unanswered question.

She called back, "Who knows why he does the things he does?"

T said, "I was hoping you might." He hung his wet clothes over the shower curtain rod, dried himself off with a towel Jenny had left on the sink, and then wrapped it around him and went to the master bedroom for his suitcase and the pajamas he remembered packing, the ones that looked like an upscale prison uniform—silk, with diagonal black and white stripes. Maura had given them to him as a birthday present several years ago. They had been the only ones he could find clean.

When he appeared before Jenny in the doorway, she said, "Oh my God, oh my God," and buried her head under the quilt. The bed rocked as she laughed.

T said, "I wasn't expecting to be seen by anyone," and got under the covers with her.

She turned over and looked out at him from an opening in the quilt. Her face was red. "Oh my God," she said. "You're so cute."

"Thank you," he said. "That's exactly how I want to be seen by a young woman, as cute."

"Oh, stop," she popped her head out from under the covers and rested her cheek on his shoulder. "You're so sensitive," she said. "You're like a sad little boy."

A small rush of anger came over T at being called a little boy. He closed his eyes and waited for it to subside. "So you feel absolutely certain Lester is coming back?"

"Absolutely," she said, and cuddled up closer to him under the blankets. "I promise, I know the guy: he's scared to death you and me are going to hook up and leave him on his own. Really, I know him." She wiggled closer to him and pushed a quilt-covered knee up over his thigh.

T saw himself for a moment as he might look to someone perched in the corner of the room, near the ceiling, or from a cinematic view, a camera angle: an older man in silk pajamas, the look in his eyes world-weary, a little cynical, with a young woman crawling over him.

Jenny said, "I never woke up in bed with a guy when I didn't, you know, the night before." She kissed him playfully on the chin.

"Obviously," T said, "you've never been married. What about Lester?"

"What about him?"

"When you lived with him for a year."

"Lester told you I lived with him for a year?" She slid down and rested her head on his stomach. "I didn't live with Lester. Well, I guess I did, technically—but it wasn't like, you know, living with him."

"It was . . . ?"

"We shared a house for a year, when I started at UTC. I got a place in town, and then I rented a room to Lester, who my family's known like since forever. So, I guess he lived with me for a year, but it was, you know: he had his room, I had mine."

"You weren't lovers? This is your freshman year in college we're talking about? You're seventeen, eighteen?"

Jenny nodded. "Lester was older. Twenty-three, I think. And he was just all this bullshit about being an actor. He was going to take a few acting classes and then go off to LA and be a star, or some such stupid shit."

"And you?" T asked. He turned so he could see her face better. The liner under her eyes had smeared into dark smudges. Her bare shoulders showed above the quilt. He reached down to stroke the thick clusters of hair cascading along her neck. She closed her eyes and leaned into his touch. "What did you want to study?" he asked. "And what happened? What happened with college?"

"Accounting," she said. "I wanted to be a CPA."

"Like Uncle Chuck?"

"Uncle Chuck has his own firm and promised to set me up soon as I graduated."

"So?" T said. "What happened?"

She hesitated, as if considering her words. Then she said, "It's a long story, and—" She was silent a moment longer. "I need to get to know you a little better." She shook her head, as if pushing a line of thought out of mind. "I made it a few weeks into my sophomore year," she continued, "and then I had to quit."

"But you were back in school now. Before—"

"I had just started again. I was just getting going on my classes."

"And the four years in between . . . ? You've been . . . ?"

"Stripping. Making money as an exotic dancer, a.k.a. stripper—but given I spend about two minutes taking my clothes off and the rest of the night walking around naked, stripper's not really—"

"Is that what you didn't want to tell me?"

"That I was a stripper? I'm not ashamed of that." She pulled his arm under her cheek and snuggled against it. "I made enough money to buy my mother's house, pay off a truckload of bills, and still have what I needed to cover college. And this is all showing it off and lap dances, nothing else."

"Stripping," T said. "You—"

"It's all acting," she interrupted. "The better actor you are, the more money you make. It's a paid exhibitionist. You dance around and stick your butt in guys' faces so they can imagine they're fucking you. It's acting. It's all fantasy."

"I'm sure," T said. "And is that what you're doing now?" He pushed her away and propped his head on his hand so that he was on his side, looking at her. "What are you doing, Jenny? This is— This is kind of silly, isn't it?"

"You think I'm silly?" She pulled the quilt to her breast, covering herself.

"I think this is silly," he said, "and, honestly, insulting to me. No?"

She seemed perplexed. She gestured with her shoulders, as if to say she had no idea what he was talking about.

"Look," he said, "just tell me what's going on. What is it really between you and Lester? What is it that you hope—"

"I told you," she said, her face reddening. "What am I supposed to do if you won't believe me?"

"The biker story?"

"It's not a story."

"Okay," T said. "Okay. How much did Lester steal?"

"Forty fucking thousand dollars," she said. She paused dramatically and then repeated herself. "He stole forty, thousand, dollars."

"And for forty thousand dollars," T said, "these people are going to kill him? And you?"

"What?" she said. "That's not enough for you?" She pulled away and sat up, still holding the blankets to her breast. "Do you know how much forty thousand dollars is to regular people, T? Do you know how impossible it is for most people to put that much money together?"

T rolled onto his back and closed his eyes, then crossed his forearms over his eyes, as if he needed a few seconds of total blindness. In the momentary silence and darkness, he noticed that it had stopped raining. He heard a single bird calling somewhere close by, a high, chirping sound, and then the odd, cackling squeal, farther away, of a crow.

"T," Jenny said, "these aren't executives we're talking about. These are tweakers. You know what tweakers are?

These are people totally fucked on crank. T?" she said. "Do you know what I'm talking about? Do you even know what crank is, T?"

"We used to call it speed," he said, from under his arms, out of the darkness. "We used to take Blackbirds in college, to stay up all night."

She laughed. "Yeah," she said. "Something like that."

T peeked out from under his arms. "So explain this to me." He sat up. "First, I'm confused. In the car you told me Lester was an ex-lover. Now you're telling me he was just a house-mate."

"Did I say that?"

"I think that's what you said."

"I think I said we weren't ever *living together,* which is a sort of semimarried thing." She waited a moment, as if she had just made a good point.

"So?"

"So, that doesn't mean we didn't get together for a little while when he was living there. That doesn't mean we didn't hook up."

"Hook up," T repeated. It was a term he had heard used before, but he had never been entirely clear on the meaning of it. "So you and Lester *hooked up* for a while."

"Exactly."

"And then, after that, he was gone; he was out of your life until—"

"I didn't say that."

"Didn't say what?"

"That he was out of my life."

"What then?" T said angrily, and immediately was taken aback by the look about Jenny's eyes, which suggested fear right under the surface. "Look," he added before she could respond, "Jenny." He touched her knee. "I don't want anything from you. I swear. I certainly don't want to hurt you. I'm just . . . seeing how I might help. But I'm not going to be some kind of a sucker. You understand what I'm saying? I want to help—but I'm not playing the sucker."

"You really believe that?" she said. The fear in her voice gave way to a hint of anger, and in that moment she seemed to shift shape as he watched, the curtain falling on one Jenny as another Jenny took the stage, this one older, much older, and not really asking a question at all. "You really believe you don't want anything from me?" she said. When T didn't answer, when he only stared at her, his eyes fastened on her eyes, she added, "Just, please don't yell at me. I know I act tough, but please don't yell at me."

T said, "I apologize if I was yelling at you."

"And then," she said, "are you sure I'm the only one who needs help around here?"

"Me?" T said. "We're talking about me now?"

"All right," she said, and looked around as if she were thinking about getting out of bed and searching for her clothes. "You want to help?" she said, and then she was suddenly playful again. "Buy me some clothes!" she yelled. "Please, T!" She folded over like a suitcase closing, her arms thrown out like someone bowing in supplication. "Please," she pleaded. "Don't make me put on those red leather tramp pants again. Please, please, please."

"I'll be happy to buy you some clothes," T said, and he shifted his body under the covers so that his leg touched her thigh, he hoped reassuringly.

For a while, they were both silent. Jenny seemed completely relaxed with her legs stretched out and her torso lying flat on her thighs in a position only possible for someone very young and very lithe. She still held the quilt to the front of her body, but her back was exposed, and T admired the way her spine defined a gentle curve before it disappeared under the covers. In the space between her shoulder blades, a subtle downward slope of skin formed a triangle where the flesh darkened slightly. He touched her there, and then took her shoulders in his hands and massaged them gently. She responded like a cat being petted. She moaned with pleasure.

After a while she said, "How come you picked us up, T? Really. I'm trying to figure that out. If it wasn't me— If it wasn't sex—"

"I don't know why I picked you up," he said quickly, brushing off the question. "Tell me about Lester, though. Why are you so sure he's coming back? Why aren't you even a little worried that we might be abandoned out here?"

T felt her shrug under his fingertips. "I suppose it's possible he took off," she said. "But hell if I know where he'd go or what he'd do."

"I thought he said Canada?"

"Yeah, with me," she said. "I'm the moneymaker. I'm the cash flow."

"And how is that again?" he said. "How is it that you're the moneymaker?"

"Stripping," she said. "There's always a strip joint someplace. It's not hard for me to find work."

"And Lester?"

"Lester's my manager."

"Manager," T said. He continued massaging her shoulders, pushing his fingers down a little deeper into the muscle. "So, he— What? Makes the arrangements? Negotiates a salary? And then he gets a percentage?"

"Mostly he does dick," she said. "But I need him to deal with the owners; otherwise—" She stopped abruptly and sighed. "It makes me tired to talk about this."

"I thought you said you weren't ashamed—"

"I'm not ashamed," she said. "But I'm not—" She sat up with her arms crossed over her breasts, still holding the quilt tightly. "Sometimes you just have to do things." She paused a moment, her eyes locked on his as if she had just told him something very important and was waiting for a response. "I'm talking about to get money," she added. "To pay for what you've got to pay for, from food to whatever. Sometimes you just have to do shit and that's all there is."

"I wasn't born wealthy," he said. "I understand about money."

"I don't think you do," she said. "Not really." She watched

him for a moment, as if trying to figure out whether or not he really did understand. Then she put her head in his lap and T returned to massaging her back. After a while she started talking slowly, as if intent on explaining things to him. "Lester's family owns a bar in Chattanooga," she said, "where my mom worked. So I practically grew up with him. He moved to Atlanta while I was still in high school, and then I didn't see him again till he showed up to rent a room from me when he enrolled at UTC. He made it through, like, one and a half semesters before he quit, and then, at the end of that year, he took off for Atlanta again, where he had a gig managing dancers, which is what he'd been doing for years, before he decided he should be an actor. After that, when I had to leave school and I needed money, I started working for him. I did that for a few years, until I had what I needed. Then I quit. I bought my mom's house. I was back in school. Then all this."

"And your mom?" T asked. He ran his fingers along her back to the base of her spine, where he pushed down hard into the flesh.

"Oh, God," she said. "That feels so good."

"Did she move someplace else?" T asked. "Your mother?"

When she didn't answer, he pushed her hair away from the side of her face so that he could see her eyes. She was looking past his thigh toward the wall as if there were something there to see. "My mother's in prison," she said. "She murdered my father. That's why I quit school. The trial took all our money."

T stroked her hair. He bent over awkwardly and kissed her back.

"I'm a murderer's daughter," she said. "Are you scared of me now?"

"Did you kill someone?" T asked.

Jenny shook her head. Her eyes remained fastened to the same empty spot on the wall. "What about you?" she said. "Do you have a secret, T?"

"Compared to you, my life's been pretty dull."

"Compared to me everyone's life's been dull. That doesn't mean you don't have a secret."

"I'm afraid not," T said. "No big secret."

She sat up and wrapped the covers around her. "I just told you that my mother murdered my father. And you're still— You're not going to tell me anything?"

T heard a hint of that other Jenny in her voice, the other, older Jenny who had appeared for only a moment. He said, "I don't know what you want me to tell you."

"I want you tell me what's going on with you," she said. "I want you to trust me a little."

T looked away from her, toward the window, where the unexpected appearance of sunlight lit up the blinds. He found it disorienting that she was asking him to trust her. He wasn't entirely convinced yet that she and Lester might not be planning to rob him—and she was asking him to trust her. What was disorienting was that he almost felt he should, and thus he found himself looking at the rose-colored blinds wondering if he would open up to her; then, to his surprise, he couldn't think of what he might open up to her about. He felt oddly as if, for the moment at least, his whole history had disappeared. "I just," he repeated himself, "I don't know what to tell you."

"Well, how about," she said, her body tensing as she leaned toward him, "how about if you start with why you've got this look like you're about ready to put a gun to your head?"

"What? What are you—"

"Oh, please, T— Why would you have picked up two characters like me and Lester?"

"I told you," he said. "I'm not really sure—"

"Well, you should think about it." She spun around out of the blankets and stomped away to the master bedroom.

T followed her. "You think I'm suicidal?" He was laughing, amused that she might think that about him. He entered the room just as she was getting into the sleigh bed.

"Oh my God!" she screamed. "These sheets are freezing!" She huddled up into a little ball.

T got into the bed behind her and wrapped his arms around her shoulders. "Jesus," he said. "You're beautiful."

She turned around and pressed herself against him. She shuddered slightly, as if trying to shake off the cold. "Where'd that come from? You think I'm beautiful when I'm mad at you?"

"It came from watching you get out of bed and walk away from me naked."

"You saw me naked last night. How come you didn't tell me I was beautiful then?"

"Didn't I?" he said. "I must have been in shock."

"From seeing me naked?"

"Must have been."

She put her arm around him and ran the palm of her hand over the silk pajamas from his shoulders to his waist and back up again, her fingers tracing a line along the middle of his body. "You must have seen it might be dangerous picking us up," she said. "I mean, we knew we must've looked bad."

"You didn't look all that bad," he said. "You looked like kids."

"Please," she said. "The way we looked, the only reason to pick us up was sex. We figured eventually some guy would come along horny enough to risk dealing with Lester."

"So I wasn't exactly what you figured. It's a big leap from there to I must be suicidal."

"That's not the whole thing," she said, and she rubbed her cheek against the silk fabric over his chest. "When I told you Lester had the pipe, you didn't seem to care. And then, not wanting to have sex with me—" She undid the top button of his pajamas and kissed him on the chest. "Not wanting to have sex with me is a very bad sign."

"What if," T said, and he touched her hair again. "What if I never was into casual sex, sex with someone you don't really know well?"

Jenny was quiet a moment, as if thinking about it. "Never met a guy like that," she said. "Is that what you're saying? It's because you don't know me well enough?"

"That," T said, "and lots of other things."

"Like what?" she asked, her manner turning coy as she undid more buttons.

"Like if I was trying not to take advantage of you."

She stopped fiddling with his pajama top, which she had pushed off his chest and tucked behind him, out of the way of her touch. "Are you kidding?"

"I'm not kidding," he answered, and he touched her shoulder, running his fingers along the curve of bone toward the center of her back. "There's no reason for you to be interested in me except that I'm in a position to help you. And I'm trying to tell you— You don't have to—"

"You don't think much of yourself," she said. "Why is that? It's not what I would have expected." When he didn't answer, she asked, "Are you fishing for compliments? Do you want me to tell you all the good things about you?"

"Jenny, please. I could be your grandfather."

"No you couldn't," she answered immediately. "My grandfather was a drunk who beat up on my father and my uncles, and wound up killing a couple of teenagers and himself driving drunk. I never heard anybody say one good word about my grandfather. That's on my father's side. On my mother's side, no one knew who he was. Not even my grandmother for sure."

T moved away from her and folded his hands under his head. "You know what I meant."

"But are you listening to me?" she asked, lifting herself over him. Her face turned red slightly, as if with a mix of anger and defiance. "I come from trash," she said. "I don't meet people like you. Ever. Or if I do, all they've got for me is a sneer."

"You're not trash," T said, meeting her eyes—though the sight of her breasts as she leaned over him had produced a rush of heat that went from his groin to his face.

"I know I'm not," she said. "But I sure am acting like it, aren't I? I'm a stripper. I'm on the run from drug dealers with an idiot who thinks he's a character in a daytime soap opera. And you don't even know the half of it. You don't know . . ." She turned away from him, a look of genuine and deep frustration in her eyes, and then collapsed onto the bed as if exhausted by the effort of trying to explain anything to him. "Forget it," she said, and she pushed her face down into the pillow before pulling the covers over her back.

T waited alongside her in silence. He could tell that the clouds were breaking up outside by the way sunlight filled the bedroom for a while and then disappeared, leaving a different room behind, one where all the colors were darker and more somber. At the moment the room was dark. It still smelled richly of wood smoke, and though the air was chilled from the night, it was warm under the bed covers. In the distance, he thought for a moment that he might have heard a car engine, but then the sound faded and left him thinking about Lester, about whether or not he'd really be coming back, and what he would do if he didn't. At worst, he figured, since his cell phone was in the console of the Rover, he'd have to walk to the nearest pay phone, where he'd call Brooke and have her wire money and arrange a rental car for him. If he couldn't reach

Brooke, he'd have to fall back on Evan, who, it was possible, might simply hang up on him. Evan claimed that growing up the only times he had ever really seen T were on vacations, that T had otherwise ignored him to the point of emotional abuse—and the trial and divorce had left him free finally to express his anger. All of which had been news to T. Maura would have been the natural second choice, but she was in London. As a last resort, he could always call one of his lawyers, though that was a particularly depressing idea.

"When I was a kid," he said, looking at the ceiling, "younger than you, I had an affair with an older woman." When Jenny remained silent, he asked, "Don't you want to know about it?"

"Not particularly," she said, her words muffled by speaking into the pillow.

He was remembering a time fishing with Carolyn near Alexandria Bay. They'd been drifting through a maze of small islands, dragging fluorescent lines through muck while the sun beat down on them relentlessly. Carolyn had taken off her top and lain with her head resting on the gunwale while her hair trailed in the water. A fishing pole was propped between her legs as she held it loosely in the palm of her hand, her other hand over the side of the boat, her fingertips playing in the water. She lay quietly in the sunlight with her eyes closed as they floated along a narrow waterway. He was sitting in the bow with his line over the side, noticing, as he usually didn't, the age lines around her eyes and across her forehead, the wrinkles along her neck and the flabby skin under her arms; and, in contrast, the youthfulness of her torso, her breasts and belly, where the skin still looked fresh and firm. She had a little girl's breasts, small and solid with puffy nipples. Her ordinarily pale chest had reddened in the sunlight. He hardly ever thought about her age. It wasn't as if they had plans to marry or have children together. It was understood that he would graduate eventually and be on his way. But as he had watched her there, so peacefully trailing her hair and fingertips in the water, he had felt something real and unnameable stir within him and then expand so that he felt filled up with it, and though he hadn't known for sure what to call it, it was a sublime feeling, a sense of timeless connection, as if they were bound to each other in some fashion that was in that instant permanent.

"What happens . . . ?" he had asked Carolyn. They'd been quiet for a long time, the only sound the breeze through the thick cattails and weeds surrounding them. His voice little and insignificant. "What happens," he repeated, louder, "if you're my one, true love?" He waited a moment and then added, "Because, you know, it feels like that. Right now, it feels like that."

"Tom," she had said, without opening her eyes. "Sweetheart," she said, her voice sleepy and listless, "you're a child."

He had gotten angry after that, and she had assured him that he needn't worry, since most of the men she knew still behaved like children.

That notion, that most men behaved like children, had occurred to him again and again throughout his life, as it was occurring to him now, in bed with Jenny Cross.

Jenny was so still he thought it was possible she might be sleeping. "This older woman told me," he said, "that men all behave like children."

"Every woman knows that," she said. "You don't have to be old."

"Why?" he asked. "What does that mean?"

She pulled herself up from the embrace of her pillow and kissed him, lightly, on the lips. "Most men are simple," she said. "They just want what they want." She thought a moment, then added, "But I don't think you're like that." She touched his thigh with the flat of her hand and then slid her palm down to his sex, which she cradled for a moment before taking him gently between her thumb and forefinger and massaging him slowly, through the silk of his pajamas. "That's what I'm kind of, piece by piece, figuring out about you," she said. "You're complicated."

T felt himself physically responding to Jenny's touch, and a part of him pulled back, wanting to resist, as another part of him acquiesced, wanting to feel and relax to her touch. "Jenny," he said, surprised a little by the way the change in his breathing affected his voice, making him sound slightly breathless. "Jenny," he repeated, "Lester told me that sex hurts you. He told me it was physically painful for you."

"With Lester it was," she said, and smiled as if she had a secret. "No," she added, and she took his pajama top off him and kissed him again on the chest. "Sometimes a girl has to find a way to let a guy down easy. You know what I mean?"

"So sex doesn't hurt you?"

Jenny's secretive smile turned wicked. "It hurts me good," she said, and she dropped down under the covers to pull off his pajamas, and then proceeded to slide up the length of his body, kissing his calves as she slowly worked her way upward.

T watched Jenny hunched over him, working so seductively with her mouth and tongue. Her kissing was artfully sensual as she moved up along his thighs—but where he should have felt desire he instead only noticed the way she was doing what she was doing; he was aware of the act of it, the performance of it, and he felt only a great, placid stillness, a well of silence, and as he watched her, his body shriveled and went slack.

"What is it?" Jenny said. She looked up from her work. "Oh, T," she said, and her voice was full of tenderness, as if she saw something in his eyes that touched her. "T," she repeated, placing the palm of her hand over his cheek gently and then lying beside him, her head burrowing into his neck. "Is it always?" she said. "Is it always like this? Is that what's going on?"

It hadn't always been like this, T thought. He hoped it wouldn't always be. But he didn't say anything. Speaking, for the moment, felt like too much of an effort. He was in a strange place. He wasn't upset, not really. He seemed, mostly, to simply not care. He felt, mostly, like a disinterested observer.

Jenny kissed his neck. "Because I wouldn't care," she said. "Really. We don't have to. You want the truth?" She stroked his hair, and seemed pleased at this chance to comfort him. In her eyes he saw a spark of eagerness. "Listen," she said, "sex has never been a big deal for me. Truly. I only wanted to because I want to be close to you." She kissed him on the temple. "Do you hear me, T?" she asked. "Do you hear what I'm saying? All I want is to be close to you."

"I hear you," T said. He added, "I don't know what's with me." He wanted to apologize, but only because he didn't want Jenny to feel responsible. He wanted to explain that he didn't think it was about her, whatever it was, but before he could figure out what to say, the cabin door opened and Lester's voice came booming happily down the hall. "Hey," he yelled. "You guys up yet?"

"Don't come back here," Jenny shouted. She wrapped her arms tightly around T when he tried to slide away from her. She held him to her and yelled, "We need some privacy, Les."

Lester ignored her and appeared in the doorway just as T pulled up the covers. In a matter of seconds Lester's expression changed from happy to worried to furious to calm. He said to T, "I see you're not having sex with Jenny again." To Jenny, he said, "I'll whip up bacon and eggs. Your favorite," and then he disappeared down the hall. From the kitchen, he yelled, "I got presents for everybody. Come on out and have breakfast."

"Damn," Jenny said. She stroked the side of T's face, running her fingers against the grain of his stubble. "I wanted to just hold you for a while."

T kissed her on the forehead. From the kitchen he heard the sounds of pots and pans clanging, and then the sizzle of fat in a frying pan. "Was the gas range working last night?" he asked.

"I don't know," Jenny answered absently. She combed the hair of his chest with her fingertips.

"He must have turned on the propane," T said, remembering a tank at the back of the cabin. "He's resourceful; you've got to give him that."

"Lester can be charming," she said. "But don't trust him, okay? He's a liar, and he's— He's just—"

"I'm not likely to trust someone," T said, "who steals my money and then comes back to announce he bought me a present."

"Actually—" she said. "Actually, that's perfect Les. It's so typical, I didn't even notice."

"What do you think he'll say when I ask him why he took my wallet?"

"I know exactly," she said. "He'll give you this look like, Is there something wrong? And if you say there is, then he'll get all hurt, like he can't believe you have a problem with him taking your wallet and spending your money. He'll turn it around like you're the cheap, ungrateful bastard and he's the poor, mistreated victim. Watch."

T sat up and gathered the strength to push himself out of bed. "I guess I'll go help him with breakfast," he said. "Then, I suppose, we should probably talk about what we're going to do, you think?"

"I don't know," Jenny said. She grabbed his arm as he started to slide away from her, and she pulled him back to kiss his shoulder. "I want more close time," she said. "You owe me, okay?"

Lester shouted from the kitchen, "Bacon's ready. Eggs'll only take a minute. You guys coming or what?" Along with his words came the aroma of coffee, and then the familiar, if long unheard, rhythm of coffee percolating in a pot.

T laughed. "I think he bought a coffee pot," he said. "I don't recall seeing one."

Jenny said, "We'll be lucky if he left us any cash."

As a way of covering his surprise at Jenny's use of *us*, T stretched and yawned. "I'd offer you a pair of my pants," he said, crossing the room toward his suitcase, "but you'd swim in them." In the suitcase, he found a pair of khakis and a black knit shirt. He sat on the edge of the bed to put them on. "I'm going to need a shower at some point."

Jenny sat up and pulled the sheets to her chest. "I'm not putting on those leather pants again," she said. "I'll walk around naked."

T found his pajama bottoms under the sheets. "You can have these if you want." He tossed them to her.

She held the pajamas to her cheek. "If it weren't for Lester," she said, "I'd prefer walking around naked."

"I'd prefer it too," he said. "In fact, I'd like to photograph you naked."

Jenny's expression changed with that, and not in the playful, seductive way he had expected. Instead, she looked suddenly worried. "What's up with the photography equipment?" she asked. Before he could answer, she added, as if a second problem had come quickly to mind, "I don't know anything about you yet. I've told you a whole lot about me, but you've—" She stopped and waited, as if hoping for him to tell her more.

"I'm an amateur photographer," he said. "With artsy ambitions."

"What's that?" she asked. "Artsy?"

"As in, to make art."

She watched him a moment in silence and then asked, "Do you have a girlfriend? Someone else? I know you said you're divorced, but—"

"No girlfriend."

"Hey!" Lester yelled. "You guys want your eggs or what? I got coffee brewing."

"It smells good," Jenny yelled back to him. When T started for the kitchen, she said, "Throw me your pajama top, sweetie, will you?"

T found the pajama top on the floor beside the bed and tossed it to her before he went out to the kitchen, where Lester was in front of the stove, turning the bacon. He wore the same heavy black boots, faded jeans, and dark T-shirt from the day before, but now his hair was pulled back into a ponytail and he was draped in a red apron with white frills that tied behind his neck and around his back. Scores of cows were sewn onto the red backdrop of the apron in various random positions so that it looked like they were floating around in red space.

Lester posed, extending one arm, greasy spatula in hand, to model the apron. "Cool?" he said. "I saw it in the window and couldn't resist it." He went back to attending the bacon.

"Lester . . ." T went around behind him and began pulling out drawers, looking for silverware. "You took my car and my wallet," he said. "And I'm assuming it's my money you spent."

"Jeez," Lester said, spinning around at the stove and crossing his arms in front of him. "A little gratefulness? A thank-you? I drove all the way into Alexandria Bay, bought food and necessary supplies, and here I am slaving in front of the stove to make you both breakfast." Before T could say anything, he added, "Are you having a good time with Jenny? Are you enjoying yourself, Tom?"

"What kind of time I'm having with Jenny's got nothing to do with you taking my car and my wallet—which, if you don't mind, I'd like back."

Lester pointed to a brown paper bag on the counter. "Why don't you get the eggs?" he said. He gestured toward T's shirt. "That's expensive, isn't it?"

"Probably," T said. "My ex bought it for me." He looked into the bag and saw two cartons of brown eggs. His wallet lay on top of the cartons. He inspected it and saw the cash was all there minus one fifty-dollar bill.

"You have one of those relationships where your wife buys all your clothes?"

"Had," T said. "What about the car keys?"

"Left them in the ignition." He pointed to a second brown bag next to the first one. "Want to grab the paper towels for me?"

T pulled out a roll of towels and brought them to the stove. He watched as Lester dropped strips of bacon onto the paper to soak up grease.

"Jenny must really like you," Lester said. "I've never known her to do it twice, night and morning, like that." He looked up from the bacon. "She must be hurting like hell. I'm surprised she can walk."

T went about gathering what he needed to make eggs.

"Does that matter to you?" Lester pressed. He watched T take a second frying pan from a cupboard. "I mean, would you care if it was, like, killing her? Or is she just, nothing, doesn't matter?"

T adjusted the flame under the frying pan and watched as a slab of butter began to melt. "You and Jenny are friends, right?" he said. "You knew her growing up? You rented a room from her while you took acting classes at UTC?"

"She told you about me?" He seemed pleased. "What else did she say?"

"She said you were friends. She said you . . . hooked up for a little while when she was renting you a room in her house. She said she worked for you as a stripper in Atlanta, that you were her manager."

Lester seemed surprised. "She told you all that?" He nodded, apparently absorbed for a moment in his own thoughts. "Did she say anything about why she worked for me?" he asked. "Did she say anything about why she needed the money?"

"What do you mean?" T cracked an egg and dropped it into the melted butter. "What do you mean, why she needed the money?"

"Nothing," Lester said. He yelled down the hall, "Jenny! The eggs are cooking!" He took three plates from the counter and put them on the table.

"Are you talking about her mother's trial?" T said. "Do you mean that she needed the money to pay for her mother's defense?"

Outside, the sun came out again and the kitchen flooded with light. T turned around to find Lester staring at him, slightly red in the face. Behind him, he heard a back-room door open, and Jenny appeared in the kitchen wearing his striped pajamas with the cuffs and sleeves rolled up.

"Hey," Lester said, "look at you. You look like an inmate in one of those old movies."

"Thank you," Jenny said. "God, it smells good in here." She wrapped her arms around T's waist and kissed him on the shoulder. "Oooh," she said, checking out the eggs. "You can cook too."

"How are you feeling?" Lester asked.

"I'm feeling fine, Lester." She leaned against T's back, her arms still wrapped around him. "By the way," she said, "What part of *Don't come back here* did you not understand?"

"Don't get bitchy," he said. "I bought you a present." He went out into the living room as T peeled Jenny's hands away from his waist and set about ladling eggs and bacon onto plates.

Jenny leaned against the stove and looked around the room. "You guys forgot the toast," she said.

"I saw bread in that bag," T said, pointing. He pulled a toaster out from under the kitchen counter and then held the plug in his hand, remembering there was no electricity. "Then again," he said, "doesn't have to be toasted."

Lester came back into the kitchen with a big smile, holding a sundress out in front of him. It was a wraparound with bright red flowers against a white background.

Jenny checked it out for a second and said, "Couldn't you find one with cows?"

Lester looked down at the floating cows on his apron and then back at Jenny. "You're not going to say thank you?"

Jenny found two cups on the counter and poured coffee for herself and T. "Thank you for the dress," she said to T. "You want milk?"

"We have any?" T asked. He took a seat at the table.

She turned back to Lester, who was holding the sundress folded over his arm and looking back at her darkly. "Did you get milk?" she asked.

"Yes, I did," Lester said. "It's in the bag."

Jenny went about pouring milk into T's coffee and then sat down to eat while Lester watched. He placed the sundress carefully on the back of his chair at the kitchen table. "Can we talk a second?" he asked Jenny. "Privately."

"T just made me these delicious eggs." She separated a piece of the white with the edge of her fork and held it up for Lester to admire.

Lester yanked her chair back from the table.

T started to get up, but Jenny quickly put a hand on his shoulder, pushing him down.

"What?" Lester said to T.

Jenny took Lester by the arm. "All right. Asshole," she said. To T she said, "Excuse us for a minute."

"Let's go outside," Lester said, looking to the front door. "Sun's out."

T watched them disappear around the front of the cabin. For a minute he considered hurrying to the bedrooms in the hope of overhearing their conversation through one of the windows, but he decided instead to go at the eggs and bacon, which were delicious. He was sopping up egg yolk with a slice of bread when he saw their shadows on the rocks through the kitchen window; then, when he stood by the counter—plate of eggs in one hand, coffee cup in the other—he saw them standing by the rocks side by side, looking down at the river and talking. He finished off his breakfast while watching them. Jenny with her long blond hair tousled by the breeze, wearing men's pajamas that wimpled and snapped in the wind, looked like she might have just stepped off the screen in one of those '50s romantic comedies, a Doris Day character, simultaneously cute and beautiful, her sexuality obvious but unthreatening—which was a striking difference from how she looked when he first saw her. He wondered about the transformation, how much of it was the clothes and how much was in his head. Lester, holding the crumpled-up cow apron in one hand, the other hand in his pocket, looked like a hometown rebel with his long hair and black boots. Sling that red guitar over his shoulder and he'd be perfect for a country western music video. Side by side, gazing out over the water, they might have been a pair of honeymooners. T watched them intently, waiting for some gesture or action that might be revealing—but they only stared out at the water a moment longer before they turned around and started back for the cabin.

They looked sad, both of them, as they walked slowly over the rocky ground, their eyes cast downward, Lester trailing a little behind Jenny. When they were close to the cabin, only a moment before they moved out of T's line of sight, Lester reached out for Jenny's hand and pulled her back to him. Jenny looked toward the cabin, as if to be sure she wasn't being watched, and then gave Lester a warm hug and fixed his hair where the wind had mussed it. He kissed her on the forehead, and they continued, hand in hand, until they disappeared from view. T sat down again at the table and sipped his coffee, and in another moment they were at the front door.

"We made up," Jenny said, sitting down to her eggs and attacking them hungrily.

Lester winked at T. "I was jealous," he said. He took a bite of egg and made a face. "They're cold."

"Still good," Jenny said, breaking a yolk with a slice of bread. "I think I was starving."

"What did you make up about?" T asked.

Jenny said, "I admitted I was being bitchy."

"And I should have asked you before I took the car and the money," Lester said. "Sorry about that."

"I told him you were worried," Jenny said. "I told him you thought he'd taken off."

"I wouldn't do that," he said. "Jenny knew I wouldn't do anything like that."

"Okay," T said. "I have my wallet back. The car's parked out front. I don't see any real harm done."

"There you go," Lester said. He took another bite of egg and then pushed the plate away.

"But we should talk about where we're going from here, don't you think?"

"Absolutely." Lester slapped the table enthusiastically. "And we should do it while we're fishing."

Jenny laughed. "He bought fishing gear and rented an outboard motor."

"You rented an outboard?"

With a grin, Lester said, "Guy at the marina owns cabin number 3. That's his boat down by the rocks."

"So you rented the outboard and the boat," T said, "and you bought fishing gear? What did you buy?"

"Couple of poles, line, bait—it's all in the boat. We're ready to go."

"And how much did this all cost?" T asked. "Because I only noticed a fifty missing, and you can't rent a boat and an outboard, outfit two people to go fishing, and buy groceries, an apron, and a sundress, all for fifty dollars. I don't care how depressed this area is."

"Well," Lester said, "I kind of used your credit cards a bit too."

T looked down at the table a moment, then back up at Lester. They both laughed.

"You said you were rich," Lester said. "I figured, what's a few hundred to a rich guy?"

"I assume both cards are back in my wallet?"

"Absolutely."

"Okay," T said. "So. We're going fishing. Is there a plan beyond that?"

"Let's talk about it," Lester said, pushing his chair back from the table.

"And you?" T said to Jenny.

"I want to lie down a bit," she said. "I thought I might warm some water in the fireplace and take a bath too. I saw a couple of big metal buckets by the propane tank."

"Nothing you won't do to get a hot bath," Lester said.

T asked, "You want some help getting the fire going again?"

"I can handle it," she said, getting up from the table. "You boys have you some fun fishing," she said, putting on her Southern accent. "Hear?" She smiled, looking suddenly tired, and turned and walked slowly out of the kitchen with T and Lester both staring after her.

T stretched out on the bed while Lester went down to the boat ahead of him—he had told Lester that he'd join him in a moment—and he found himself wondering what Alicia would say if she could somehow see him here, if somehow she could walk like a ghost around the cabin and see Jenny in the bathroom and him in the bed taking a moment for himself before going fishing with Lester. No doubt she would be perplexed. She would have a hard time figuring out T taking up with Jenny and hanging out with Lester. In those last years before the divorce, she had come to see T as a simple bore. The marriage was already dead those last few years, though T hadn't known it. He thought it was only changed and quieted after the children had grown and gone off to start their own lives. Free from the responsibility of children and still relatively young, Alicia had gone back to work in the city, acting when she could, volunteering where needed, keeping busy, spending most nights in Manhattan. While T did what? He could hardly remember. He called people on the phone. He set up appointments. He visited sites, hired workers, negotiated contracts. He watched football. That he remembered. He watched a lot of football. Dinner and a movie or a play was a big night out. The guy who might spend a day wandering through a museum, that guy was long gone. Sundays he spent mostly on the couch watching games. Weekdays he was busy. Really, he was always busy. When he thought back to himself in those years, he saw a man on the phone, a man in traffic, a man going somewhere or coming back, while his wife was somewhere else, doing something else, which was fine with him because it meant she was entertained and thus he didn't have to worry about keeping her happy, which he was too busy to worry about, busy doing a lot of things that would all come, only a few years later, to nothing.

When she came to see him in Salem, after the divorce, she had rushed into an old argument, intent, it seemed, on delivering a final blow. "You're a void," she told him. "You're a vacuum, an abyss, a black hole." T had long ago gotten used to her overblown rhetoric, her dramatic posturing. It was to be expected when married to an actress. She was making the argument she had made for many years, that there was something lacking in him, that he was directionless, that having no desire of his own, he relied on others to shape his life, to give him purpose. It was an argument that used to infuriate him. He had built a series of businesses from scratch to the point where they were making millions—money that she had no problem whatsoever spending. What was that, building those businesses, if not ambition? That took work. Hard work.

The kitchen wallpaper in Salem pictured red and yellow blossoms on a white background. He had made a note to tear it down as soon as he moved in, and of course never did. Alicia in her New-York-artist black—black shoes, black pants, black top—gave the impression of being superimposed over the kitchen wall, a kind of digital special effect. She was thin, as always, but her skin seemed more vibrant, more healthy than he remembered. She was still an attractive woman. Not a stunning beauty, but beautifully interesting in her looks, her angular, lithe body, her newly blond hair, which was thin and streaked with platinum.

"A black hole?" he asked from his seat at the table, resting his head on his hand, looking up at her where she stood over him with her hands on her hips. "Really?"

"Yes," she said. "A black hole." She seemed nervous—jittery with a kind of anxious energy that suggested she was scared, scared about being there in Salem, in his house, alone with him. Yet she had made the long drive. She had called him. She said she needed to talk. Then, within moments of coming through the door, before they even made it out of the kitchen, she exploded into her lecture. T looked up at her. She stared back at him. Her look said she was frightened. Her eyes filled with tears.

He said, "Don't you think you're being slightly dramatic?"

"No," she said, her voice dropping to a whisper. "Look, T," she said, "I don't know what happened, but at some point, I stopped being a real person to you. Actually, I don't know that I was ever— To you, that I was ever—"

T said, "I don't know what you're talking about, Alicia."

"I think maybe," she went on, as if still working through the problem, "it's women— For you— We're like place mats, in some ways, like accessories."

T wondered if he had heard her correctly. "Women are like place mats to me? Is that what you just said?"

"You don't see," she answered. "At least you got to be that way—or maybe you never did. I don't know. But I know, eventually, you couldn't see anybody but yourself." She wiped her eyes and took a seat beside him. She spoke as if patiently explaining his own life to him. "You married Brooke because she offered you money and a way to live after you'd been drifting for years. After Brooke walked out on you, you married me because I gave you a family and, again, a way to live. And then you just disappeared. You went away, T. You left it to me to run everything that wasn't business, that wasn't work. You used me, T. To raise your daughter, to— Can you tell me one vacation you planned? One trip that was your idea? One move that you wanted? Anything? Any activity, any anything in our life that you initiated? Can you tell me anything at all that was yours?"

"Maura," he said. "Maura was mine."

"Maura was Brooke's!" she shouted. "Until I took over. Have you noticed she's more in touch with me than she is with her own father? Why do you think that is? She calls me twice a week from London. How often does she call you, Tom?"

T looked down at his belly and closed his eyes. He laid his hands flat on the tabletop, as if to steady himself.

"And Evan," she went on, leaning closer to him. "Why is it that Evan won't even talk to you? Don't you even wonder about such things?"

"Could it be," T said reasonably, meeting her eyes, "could it be that they both, thanks to you, think I'm a child molester?"

Alicia nodded and was silent. Her look suggested a deep sadness at the subject being raised. "I didn't download that picture," she said. "I thought you were just a monster of indifference, a monster of blindness, but when I saw that picture? When I saw that picture, I saw what a beast you really were. I almost died when I saw it. I think a part of me did die. I never would have believed—"

"Oh, shut up," T said. He got out of his chair and gestured toward the back of the kitchen. "Do you see an audience? It's just me and you, Alicia, and you know goddamn well I'm no pervert, I'm no pedophile. That's an ugly, ugly lie that you used to destroy me."

"Now who's being dramatic?"

"You think that's dramatic?" He pointed out the window, toward the mountain. "I'm in fucking exile here!" he shouted. "I'm lost. I don't have a clue—" He stopped when he heard what he was saying and saw the pity in Alicia's eyes. "Fuck you," he said calmly. "You try having your life ripped away from you in a matter of months and see whether or not you feel lost."

"Okay," Alicia said. She closed her eyes for a moment, as if pulling herself together. "I'm sorry. I'm sorry for what's happened to you. I came here to tell you that."

"Thank you," he said. "That's very kind of you." He pulled out a bottle of chianti from its rack atop the refrigerator. "Will you have a glass?" he asked. She sat quietly at the table, not even looking at him. "I will," he said, and went about opening it. He pulled a wine glass down from the cabinet above the microwave. "Why are you really here?" he asked. He held the glass out to her. "Are you sure you don't want some?" he asked. "It's a good chianti."

"To tell you what happened," she said, ignoring the offer.

T poured his wine and then leaned back against the sink.

"I fell in love," she said. "I found a man who had something to give back to me, someone who could fill me up and not drain me."

"Victor? The guy you're living with now?" he said. "The failed actor? You came here to tell me you love him?"

She looked up at T then and leaned closer. She spoke carefully, as if intent on being understood. "He knows how to love a woman without draining her," she said. "He knows who he is and what he wants from this life. He doesn't *use* women."

"Good for him," T said. "Did you really come all the way here just to tell me that? Really?"

"You're not getting it," she said. "You're not hearing me."

T considered what Alicia might be trying to tell him. "Before?" he said. "Are you saying— You were with him before—"

"For a long time before," she said. "More than a year." She looked furious. "What does it say, T, that you never had an inkling?"

T's stomach was suddenly queasy, the way it got when he looked down from a great height. Along with the one incriminating picture he had downloaded, the one Alicia had turned him in for, the court had found other photographs, some more shocking than anything he had ever come across on his own. Where they came from had baffled him. All he could tell the court was that he had no way to explain their presence on his hard drive. He assumed that somehow the computer had downloaded them automatically, by itself, when he visited pornography sites, which he admitted to occasionally doing. It was how he found the one damning picture. He had browsed porn sites on occasion, and he knew computers could do such things, cache pictures, save them in hidden places. He'd read stories of hackers hijacking people's hard drives and using them for their own purposes. He thought perhaps something like that might have happened. Some freak had gotten his address from the one site he visited and then hijacked his computer and used it to store child pornography. It was the only explanation he could imagine. The court discounted it. They said he had to have been the one who downloaded the images. "Did you—" he asked Alicia. "Did you put those pictures there?"

"You put that picture there," she said. "That little girl. I found it. I found it right on your desktop."

"But the others," he said. "The other—"

She nodded. "I was with Vic," she said. "He knows computers. We were looking for your financial records. I had already decided to divorce you, and I didn't trust you to be honest. When we found that picture—"

Leaning against the sink, T felt simultaneously heavy and light. His body was too heavy to move and yet it felt as though it might at any moment float up from the floor and drift away.

"It was a terrible thing to do," she said. She wiped away a tear, roughly, with the back of her hand. "But that picture *was* yours. You *did* look at that filth. We went back to the exact same site you had downloaded it from—and we just downloaded some more."

T said, "I just— The one picture . . ."

"That's what you did, ignoring me, leering at—"

"I was only—" T started to explain himself but stopped abruptly when he realized what he was doing. "I never as much as dreamed it," he said calmly. "All through the trial, it was a mystery. It never even occurred to me."

"All the years you took," she said. "I was nothing to you. None of us were." She drew a quick, sharp breath. "I'm not sorry. I'd do it again."

T opened the kitchen door and then walked away from it, indicating that she should leave.

At the door, Alicia regained her composure. "It was wrong," she said, "but I'd do it again, to get away from you, to make a new start." She added, just before she turned to leave, "And you *did* download that picture."

T couldn't look at her. He went into the living room with his glass of wine. He was sipping it and staring at the wall when he heard her drive away.

The sound of running water came from the bathroom in the cabin, and T pushed himself up to his feet. He looked out the bedroom window to the river, where the sun was shining brightly now on water that was calm and blue. It was heating up outside, turning into a gorgeous summery fall day. T took a deep breath and exhaled slowly, shaking off the weight of memory, and then left the cabin and started down the embankment to the river.

Lester pushed the boat out into the water and then nearly capsized it when he jumped in. It was sunny and hot, and he had taken off his jeans and boots in order to keep them dry while he waded among the rocks untying the bow and stern lines from a pair of submerged anchors. T had watched him do this, interested in the proprietary manner with which he approached the boat in particular and the whole fishing outing in general. As the boat drifted away from the rocks with T sitting quietly in the bow, Lester pulled himself up from his knees, where he had landed awkwardly, grabbing at both gunwales to steady the boat. He took a seat by the outboard and went about pulling on his pants. T was finding it hard not to look at his black bikini underwear, the crotch of which pictured the striped head of a roaring tiger.

"One of the girls gave them to me," Lester said as he stood to zip up.

"The girls?"

Lester looked as though he thought about explaining for a brief second and then decided against it. He handed T a fishing pole. "You know how to fish?"

"I used to fish right here," T said, taking the pole. "I lived in Syracuse and we'd come out here to go fishing."

"No kidding? Right here? This very spot?"

"It's possible. It was a long time ago."

"So you can tie your hook on, and bait and cast and all that stuff?" Lester placed a battered tackle box on the center thwart, between them. "Guy loaned us this," he said, referring to the tackle box. "Look at all this shit."

The box opened to reveal three tiers divided into a dozen compartments, each containing an assortment of lures, hooks, and various colorful tackle. Lester picked up a sparkling red plastic worm and observed it for a second. "How are you supposed to catch anything with this?" he said. "Where's the hook?"

"Rubber worm," T said. He found the appropriate hook and threaded it through another worm, a purple one. He held it up for Lester to see.

Lester spit over the side of the boat. "We never used fake worms," he said. "They any good?"

"I seem to remember they were pretty good," T said. "Let's see." He tied his line to the hook, fastened a pair of split weights toward the end of the line, and tossed it into the water.

They both watched and listened as black line spooled off the reel.

"We mostly just used bait and a few artificial lures," Lester said, his eyes fastened to the fishing line where it disappeared into the water. "My dad used to take me all the time when I was little. We'd go to the lake mostly. We'd catch bream."

"Never heard of bream," T said. He flipped the bail arm back on the reel as he felt the weights hit bottom. "What kind of fish are they?"

"Fish fish," Lester said. "I don't know." He went about tying a clip to his line and putting on a small silver spoon.

The boat drifted slowly, parallel to the shore. T watched the red cabins slide past as they came up on cabin 6. The bright brass number nailed to the back door caught the sunlight and gleamed.

"We used to have a cabin on the lake," Lester said dreamily. He leaned back and expertly cast his spoon out toward the center of the river and then reeled the line back in slowly, moving the tip of the pole occasionally to change the action of the spoon.

"You look like you know what you're doing."

"Like I said . . ." He pulled in the spoon and then cast it out again. "I always liked fishing with lures. My dad was strictly a hook-and-worm fisherman. That and a trotline. Man loved to run a trotline out behind the cabin, drink beer all night, and get up in the morning to see what he caught."

T could feel the weights on the end of his line bumping along the bottom. They caught on something, providing him a surprising jolt of adrenaline before he recognized the constant pull as a snag. He jerked the pole slightly and it came loose. The jolt was surprising because he didn't imagine that he gave a damn about catching a fish. In fact, he hoped he didn't, as he had no desire to go through the slimy process of pulling his hook out of a fish's mouth. "So a trotline's what?" he said. "Like a net?"

Lester laughed and said, "You are not a Southern boy. A trotline's a bunch of plastic milk jugs or soda bottles or what-not tied together with a rope, and the bottles have hooks and lines tied off them."

"Where's the sport in that?"

Lester shrugged. "Don't know about sport. My daddy loved to go out there in the morning, though; see what he caught."

"He doesn't anymore?"

"Died of a heart attack when I was in middle school."

"Sorry to hear that."

"Been a long time." Lester reeled the spoon in, unclipped it, and searched through the tackle box for another lure.

"You sure that outboard works?" T asked. "I'd hate to have to row back to the cabin."

"It'll work," Lester said, preoccupied with examining the various bright-colored jigs and spoons and fish lures. "Besides," he added, "I'd do the rowing." He looked up from the tackle box. "I'm the young man here."

"I'm hardly decrepit."

"No. But you are old." He picked out a marmalade-orange diving fish and clipped it to his line. "It kind of pisses me off," he said, holding the fish in one hand and the pole in the other, hesitating before casting. "It kind of pisses me off that you get the girl."

"Is that what happened?" T said. "Did I get the girl?"

"Look like it to me." He cast the lure out behind him, toward the rocks on the shore. "You're older than my father would be if he were alive," he said. Then he added, "We're drifting nice. We should catch something." He pulled the lure back in and then cast it out again. He nodded toward T's fishing pole. "Ain't it kind of boring, just letting your line drag in the water like that?"

"I'm okay," T said. "It's the way old guys like to fish."

Lester grinned and gave the tip of his pole a jerk.

T said, "I'm actually more interested in hearing what you have to say than I am in fishing."

"Say about what?" Lester asked. "About you?"

"About what you want," T said. "About what we're doing here."

Lester spit over the side of the boat again. "You want to get right down to business, huh? You don't want to fish a little bit? Relax?"

"We're fishing," T said. "Tell me what happened with the drugs."

"With the coke?"

"I thought Jenny said speed."

"Crank?" Lester said. "What did she say?"

"Why don't you just tell me?"

Lester pulled back slowly on his fishing line, as if testing the feel of the lure. "If you get a bite," he said, "you need to jerk the tip hard, set the hook."

T nodded and watched, waiting for Lester to get around to the story.

"Basically, I screwed up," he said. "Guy I share a house with, named Lyle, hooked up another guy, named Short Willie, with some college kids from UT who were selling what was supposed to be, I don't know, some kind of supercrank, or some such shit like that."

T said, "The guy's name is Short Willie? Are you putting me on?"

Lester looked perplexed for a moment. On the shore, near the rocks, a blue heron waded in the water. The boat drifted out farther from the shoreline. "His name's Willie," Lester said, "and he's only maybe five four, five five. But he's built like a tank, and he even thought you were thinking what you're thinking about his name, you'd wind up buried someplace in the Smokies, along with a lot of other guys."

"Really? He's that bad, huh?"

"Shut the fuck up and listen. Okay? Tom? Aloysius?"

T put his fishing pole down, wedging the butt under the rowing thwart. He crossed his arms.

Lester tossed his lure toward the shoreline angrily, let it sink a moment, and then began reeling it in. "The money was in the house, forty thousand, sitting there in a cardboard box. I set up a deal with some Mexicans to buy coke with the forty, and then I was going to sell it to this rich asshole I know for almost twice that. Guy's name's Walter Lyse. His family owns half of Chattanooga."

"And the Mexicans ripped you off."

"I had good reason to believe they were trustworthy," Lester said, pulling the lure in and snapping it out again with a flick of his wrist. "Walter I've been dealing drugs to since I was in grade school. The whole thing should have been over in less than an hour, the money back in the box; I'm about thirty thousand dollars richer."

"What happened with the Mexicans?" T said. "Describe it to me. Where did you meet them? What did the place look like? How'd they rip you off? Did they have guns? How many of them were there?"

"Fuck," Lester said. "You think I could make this shit up? I met them at the Super 8 off I-24. Ordinary motel room with a television hidden inside a dresser across from a king-size bed and a little round table by a window and pictures of trains on the wall, if I remember right. I walked in, said something brilliant like, "Hey, dudes." There were three guys in the room, two sitting facing me on the bed, one of the guys on the bed with a blue do-rag, the other guy bald. I'd guess they were all three of them in their thirties. The one who opened the door for me—I had the money under my arm in a shoebox—looks out into the hall, doesn't even close the door. He puts a knife to my throat, takes the box. On the way out the door, the bald guy kicks me in the balls so hard I swear to God I go blind for a minute. While I'm on the ground moaning, one of them frisks me, and that's it. By the time I can stand up, they're gone."

T picked up his pole again and began taking in line. Behind him, the first cabin was slipping away.

Lester said, "You're looking doubtful, T. You're looking like you don't believe me. What do you want me to do? Describe their tattoos? Fine. The guy with the knife—"

"What I'm finding hard to believe," T interrupted, "is that you'd go into such a thing with no protection. No guns. Nobody with you. That's not how it is in the movies. Plus, the huge discrepancy in what you're buying it for and selling it for. These things, they don't—"

"I told you, I screwed up." He pulled in his line and turned to look at the outboard as if he were considering firing it up. "Still," he added, "I had reason to believe I'd have no problem with the Mexicans. And I don't carry a gun. People that carry guns get shot. I couldn't bring anybody else into it because if it ever got back to Willie, I'd be dead. And also, I was greedy and didn't think I needed anybody else. So. That's what happened."

"All right," T said. "Tell me one more thing."

"We're heading out toward the middle," Lester said. He looked back and forth quickly from the shore to a big island in the middle of the river. "What do you think? We weren't having any luck along the shore . . ."

"Why not?" T said. "Just keep your eyes out for the big ships. They can sneak up on you."

Lester shrugged and turned his attention to the tackle box, picking up and examining a silver jig with a blue feather.

"How did you know the Mexicans?" T said. "Just explain that to me, and then we can drop it. How did you know these Mexicans? Where did you meet them? Why did you think there'd be no trouble?"

Lester didn't answer for a second. He seemed to flush slightly.

"Because," T pressed, "*Mexicans*—it's awfully generic, don't you think?"

"Look," Lester said, "it's what happened. I didn't know them. I knew of them. From some guys I know. Guys connected with my dancers."

"Guys you know . . ." T said. He felt his fishing line come up off the bottom as they moved out into the deeper water, and he flipped the bail to let it play out again. "Listen," he said, "so? What? What is it you'd like me to do?"

"You can loan us the money to pay back Short Willie." Lester dropped the silver jig over the side of the boat and watched it in silence a moment as the blue feather disappeared into the depths. "I mean," he continued, "I'm not going to bullshit you and say we have any idea when or how we can pay you back, or anything like that. We're both fucked for money right now. But, you know, at some point, when things turn around in my life—"

The current was picking up as they moved farther from the shore. T looked away from Lester and watched the line of cabins grow smaller. "So I'd give you a check for forty thousand dollars," he said, "and you'd, what, go find this Short Willie and give him his money back? You and Jenny would take the money and go back to Chattanooga?"

"Checks don't work in my world," Lester said. "You'd need to get us the cash."

"So, cash," T said. "You take the cash and you and Jenny'd go back to Tennessee?"

"We'd have to get the money back to Willie somehow. We'd make some kind of deal, I guess." Lester's expression turned genuinely worried as he apparently considered how to give the money back. "Fuck knows what's happened to Lyle," he said. "He didn't have anything to do with my shit, but— If Lyle's still around, we might could go through him."

"To get the money back to Short Willie?"

"If Lyle's not rotting in the Smokies somewhere."

"So you're thinking," T said, "something like: Monday morning we all get up bright and early and go find a bank in town. I make arrangements to have forty thousand wired to me. And then what? I give you the money and you and Jenny take off for Chattanooga? How? You want me to give you the Rover too?"

"Actually," Lester said. "I was actually hoping you'd part with fifty or sixty thousand. That'd give me and Jenny a little something to get our lives back together with after we paid back the forty."

"Fifty or sixty thousand."

"How much is that to a rich guy?" Lester asked. "I mean, is that a whole lot of money?"

"And this is a loan, of course."

"Like I said . . ."

Lester seemed to have forgotten about fishing. His line dragged behind the boat, as did T's. They watched each other in silence while the boat drifted toward a big island close to the center of the river. A small section of a shingled roof was visible above the island's tree line.

"Let's say I get you fifty thousand," T said. "And let's say we make some sort of arrangements for transportation, since I'm assuming you don't want to hitchhike with a bag full of money. Then what you're saying is: you and Jenny would go your way, and I'd go mine? Is that right? Is that what you're thinking?"

Lester turned his attention to his fishing pole, reeling in the line before setting the pole down beside him, as if all pretext of fishing was over. "I might could try to talk Jenny into staying," he said, "if that makes a difference. I mean, I know she's got a thing for you. The only reason she'd want to go at all is to put her stuff back together at home. I mean, my understanding is she's got a thing for you. That's right, isn't it? You two hit it off?"

"Before she what?" T said. "Before she came back to Virginia with me?"

"That's all Jenny," Lester said. "I got nothing to say about what Jenny does."

"Fifty thousand is a lot of money," T said. "I'm not that rich."

"Sixty thousand be better," Lester said.

T said, "You think that's something Jenny's considering? Coming with me?"

"I don't know," Lester said. "It could be. She's got a house in Chattanooga. She tell you about that?"

"She told me it got wrecked by bikers. You didn't mention anything about bikers, did you?"

"That's Short Willie." The boat drifted into the shadow of the island, and Lester leaned over the side to look past T. Beyond a rocky promontory, the island curved gently inward to a stretch of narrow beach. He leaned over the outboard, tilted the engine, and locked it in place with the propeller out of the water. "His crew's about eight guys," he continued, "but they're hooked up with bikers 'cross the country. It's like a big crank conglomerate."

T watched the island come up at them. The house on the other side of the trees was completely hidden. The sky had turned a creamy blue with only a few scattered clouds to block the sun. "You do crank?" he asked.

"Rarely. Stuff'll kill you in a heartbeat."

"What about Jenny?"

Lester looked at him as if he were out of his mind. "Look," he said. "Jenny's got it all over most people. How much she tell you about herself?" He cast an annoyed glance at T, as if frustrated at having to talk to him about Jenny. "She was doing fine," he said, "till her mother blew her father away. She tell you that? Woman put a shotgun in her husband's mouth and pulled the trigger. Turned the back of his head into tomato paste."

"Colorful," T said.

"You think so? Did Jenny tell you she practically paid for the whole trial herself?"

"She mentioned—"

"Jenny'll talk about the way men look at her; she's got this ability to peg a guy dead-on after one look. It's unbelievable. Do you understand what I'm saying? People, because of where she comes from, they miss how special the girl is. They don't get Jenny, most people."

Beneath them, the water was rapidly growing shallow. The bottom vegetation, long fields of green weeds and thin clouds of moss, wavered in the watery light. The island, thick with skinny pine trees and tangled scrub, loomed up over the boat, blocking any view of the river beyond it. Without explanation, Lester took off his pants and jumped acrobatically out of the boat feet first into the water, which came up to his chest, soaking his T-shirt. "Son of a bitch," he said. He looked shocked.

T said, "Water's usually deeper than it looks."

"Thank you," Lester said. He took off his shirt and tossed it sopping into the boat.

"Any particular reason you're in the water?" T asked.

Lester went around to the bow without answering. He took the bow line in hand and pulled the boat behind him as he waded to the beach. The sandy part near the shore was at most a foot or two deep, and when the bow was up against it, T stepped out and helped Lester pull the boat out of the water, up into the scrub.

"Son of a bitch," Lester said again. He took off his underwear and wrung it out, water pouring in a stream out of the tiger's mouth, then laid it on a rock in the sun and sat down on the sand with his knees up. Except for a slight paunch, he was built thick and solid, with the kind of biceps and chest and shoulder muscles that only came from lifting weights. A colorful tattoo of a Bengal tiger prowling a green forest covered a good portion of his right shoulder blade. "You should pull in your line," he said, gesturing toward the back of the boat.

T looked behind him, in the direction of the house, and decided it was probably empty at this time of year, as were most of the vacation houses on these islands after Labor Day. He took his pole from the boat and sat next to Lester. "You must think," he said, "that you've really stepped in shit, Lester."

"Why's that?" Lester said, suddenly pensive, barely interested in T.

"Here you are one day, broke, hitchhiking with your girlfriend; the next day, you're talking to some asshole with money actually seems to be considering giving you fifty thousand dollars. In cash."

"Sixty," Lester said. "Jenny's not my girlfriend."

"But I am an asshole with money."

"You said it, dude."

"Why should I give you fifty grand, Lester? Really?" He started slowly pulling in line. Virtually all of the reel had played out.

"For Jenny's sake," he said. "Girl's been through a nightmare the last few years." Lester turned to look at him. "How much she tell you about her mother?"

"All she said was the murder. I didn't ask for details."

Lester turned back to the river and was quiet a moment, as if gathering his thoughts. "Jenny's whole family," he said, "is her mother and father and two uncles. That's the whole thing. The grandparents are dead, no cousins or anything like that. Then her uncle—the guy whose guitar it was, the one we got with us—he drowned himself in the lake. That was like the beginning. Jenny was close to him. A couple of years after that, her mother kills her father. Then they send her mother away for life without parole, this after Jenny put everything she had into trying to save her from that. Probably did save her from the death penalty."

"I don't doubt any of that," T said. He had stopped reeling in line. "I think she's an extraordinary girl."

"She's got a body to die for, don't you think?"

T went back to slowly reeling in line.

"That was actually a kind of sick joke," Lester said.

"What was?"

"Came out during the trial," he said, "that her mother killed her father because of her, because of Jenny."

T stopped reeling again. He put the pole down between his legs.

"Turned out her uncle, Chuck, guy whose cabin this is, been taking pictures of Jenny from the time she was a baby. I'm talking three, four years old."

"What do you mean by pictures?"

"You know what I mean," Lester said. "I'm not talking about family snapshots."

"From the age of three or four?"

"Jenny says long as she can remember, he'd get her alone, give her some present. She didn't know. He'd tell her to take off her clothes, what did she know? When she got to be older, it was just . . . Uncle Chuck. She liked the presents."

"So this went on . . . ?"

"Till she was fifteen, sixteen."

"And only the pictures?"

"Far as I know."

T picked up the pole again and looked out at the water a while before continuing to reel in line. "And what—" he asked after thinking a moment. "What did that have to do with her mother killing her father?"

"Sick shit," Lester said. He picked up a rock off the beach and skimmed it over the water. "Babs found the pictures, shitloads of them, in the basement with all the rest of Johnny's porno."

"This is her parents?" T said. "Babs and Johnny?"

Lester nodded. "Come out during the trial, though, that Johnny wasn't Jenny's real father. It was some other guy; no one knew." He paused, as if remembering something, then added, "Well, Johnny knew. He married her anyway, when she was knocked up with this other guy's kid."

"But Jenny didn't?"

Lester shook his head. "That cleared up a whole lot of questions, though—since no one could ever figure out how an ugly character like Johnny Cross could ever have anything to do with a girl looks like Jenny. Or even Babs, who was gorgeous before she put on like a hundred extra pounds."

"So she found the pictures and just went and got the shotgun."

"Exactly." Lester pointed to T's line, which had suddenly grown taut. "You snagged on something?"

"Looks like it," T said. He tugged at the line, and it gave a little.

"Babs testified she saw the pictures and imagined him jerking off over Jenny, went and got the shotgun, found him sleeping, stuck the gun in his mouth, and pulled the trigger."

T yanked back hard on the fishing pole, intending to either free the snag or snap the line. He was surprised when the pole jerked back with several hard snaps in succession, pulling line off the reel in short squeals.

"Sum' bitch," Lester said. "You got something."

T yanked at the pole, hoping the line would snap, but the creature on the other end yanked back harder, bending the pole in a near U. "What test is on here?" he asked.

"I don't know," Lester said. "Why? You worried it'll snap?"

"I wish." T stood and put his whole body into pulling back on the pole. "It's an eel," he said. "I hope there's a knife in that tackle box."

Lester got up and reached into the boat for the tackle box. He seemed to have forgotten he was naked as he bent over and mooned T. "How do you know it's an eel?" He came up from the tackle box with a filleting knife in hand.

"Look at the way the line is twisting." He gestured toward the water, where the line was spinning in tight circles as T reeled it in.

"Can you eat eels?"

"Not these," T said. He and Carolyn had caught several of the long, snake-like creatures on their fishing trips. They were notoriously toxic from all the chemicals scrounged off the bottom of the lake. Signs were posted at all the boat ramps warning against eating them.

"How come?" Lester waited with his hands on his hips. He watched the water with fascination.

"They're bottom-feeders," T said. "They're full of garbage."

T jumped back away from the eel as he yanked it out of the water and onto the sand. It was unlike any eel he had ever seen. Rather than the long, snake-like creature he was familiar with, this eel was short, not much more than a foot, and thick, a good four or five inches at the head, tapering down to an inch or less. Its skin was the color of wet sand, and it had two otherworldly pink eyes. "God, that's disgusting," T said as the eel frantically spun and twirled on the beach, making a mess of the fishing line.

Lester knelt alongside it with the filleting knife. When he tried to hold it with one hand so he could cut the line with the other, it spun so violently that it leaped onto his knees, spinning over his crotch and onto his stomach before he could jump away from it. "Son of a bitch," he said. The eel had left a thick layer of slime everywhere it had touched him. He tried to wipe it away with the back of his hand. "It's all over me," he said. Then he stepped on the eel, holding it still long enough to cut the line close to the hook before he kicked it back into the water, where it instantly disappeared. "Thing looked like a big corkscrew," he said.

T said, "Looked like the slug from hell."

Lester took his wet T-shirt from the boat and waded out into the water. "You see those pink eyes?" He wiped at the slime with his shirt and then held it to his nose. "Stinks," he said.

T slid his pole under a thwart and then went around to the bow to push the boat back into the lake. "I'm ready to go."

Lester grabbed the boat by the transom and pulled it the rest of the way into the water as T leaped into the bow.

"How come I do all the hard work?" Lester said, retrieving his tiger underwear from its rock.

"Because I'm the old guy," T said.

Lester said, "You think that's it?" He waded out into the water again and then pulled himself into the boat, where he dropped the engine down and squeezed a rubber bulb attached to a hose that ran from a red gas container.

"Or it could be because I've got the fifty thousand you want," T said.

"Sixty," Lester said, and then started the engine with a single pull on a black cord.

At the back entrance to the cabin, T stopped a minute and watched Lester drifting a few feet out from the shore, standing upright in the boat and casting his line toward the rocks with what looked like intense concentration. He was barefoot and shirtless, wearing only his jeans. From where T looked down at him, with a frontal view, in bright sunlight, he appeared boyishly innocent, his hair wet and pulled back, his chest and arms muscled and almost completely hairless. From the back, T imagined, with his long hair pasted against his neck and the orange Bengal tiger prowling the green woods of his shoulder blade, he'd cut a different picture.

It was obvious to T, when Lester dropped him off on the rocks and told him he wanted to fish a little more, that he was intentionally being left alone with Jenny, and he felt anxious now as he was about to enter the cabin. He felt as if he and Lester had negotiated a deal and now he was here to sign the contract—though in fact they had agreed upon exactly nothing. They hadn't said another two words to each other on the trip back across the lake, and Lester had dropped him off with a simple "I'm going to fish a little more." Still, he felt as though something had changed, as though Jenny were his for the taking now, and he hesitated outside the cabin. He imagined her in bed, still warm from the bath, waiting for him, and the thought made him flush a little as he recalled the image of her throwing off the quilt and walking naked away from his bed, that shock of blond hair bouncing over a catlike harmony of muscle and skin—and there was something more than that, more than her body alone, her youth alone, that he could feel pulling at him. It was as if, when he was with her, with Jenny, there was something in the interaction that made him feel . . . He couldn't find the words for it. And maybe it wasn't even that she made him feel it but only that she made him feel the possibility of it. She made him feel . . . comfortable, or at ease, or maybe just more human. Whatever it was, he realized it was something he hadn't felt in a long time—and that thought, that he hadn't felt that way in a very long time, seemed somehow dangerous.

Rather than enter the cabin immediately, he found a long, flat rock out of Lester's view and lay back in the sunlight. After a moment, he took off his shirt to better enjoy the warmth of the rock on his back and the sun on his chest. He wondered if there weren't something special about the Saint Lawrence River and the Thousand Islands, at least where he was concerned. So much had happened for him here in the past, and now, upon his first return in more than thirty years, this. It was almost a reversal of the former situation, and he had the odd sense of time warping and bending back on itself, casting him into the 1960s again, only in another dimension, where all the details were reversed. Then he was a boy, here with an older woman. Now he was an older man, here with a girl.

He understood, in retrospect, that he had been in love with Carolyn Wald. He had traveled upstate to see her only a few days before he married Brooke and found that she had aged considerably in the four years since he had graduated from Syracuse and gone off to travel in Europe on his own for a few months, as was customary for hippies back then. He had contacted her on average once or twice a year after his return to the States, and she had always refused to see him. He had called her from San Louis Obispo, where he had spent almost a year living on a commune with a moody Chinese girl who had changed her name from Kim to Lost Feather. He had called her from Wallkill, New York, where he had spent another year working on a horse farm, living with a sculptor named Josephine, a woman he remembered as intelligent, talented, and neurotic. And he had phoned her several times from Manhattan, where he had gone through several inconsequential relationships while working an assortment of temporary jobs. She had refused to see him every time, once telling him he had never meant anything to her and asking him not to call again.

It wasn't until he told her that he was marrying Brooke and needed to see her one more time that she had agreed, and when he arrived at her house in Syracuse after an absence of four years, he felt like a supplicant, though he had no idea what it was that he wanted.

He guessed, thinking back now on how much she had aged, that she had probably already begun her struggles with cancer. Her obituary claimed she had been battling it for many years. He knew, really, almost nothing about those years—but cancer would explain why she had refused to see him, and why she seemed thinner than he remembered, her face more pinched and lined with wrinkles. Still, once he was inside her house again, inside her enclave of bookcase-lined walls with art everywhere—standing sculptures, hanging paintings, floating mobiles—where colorful displays of fresh-cut flowers scented the air, he quickly stopped noticing her age and found himself caught up again in her enthusiasm for poetry and art, for literature, for culture, for science, politics, history; caught up in their typical lopsided conversations where the sound of her voice worked on him like a spell. Just as was the case when he was her student, all he had to do was listen. Even now, lying shirtless on a rock in sunlight, remembering back more than thirty years, that vivid sense came back to him, the sense he had in her presence, listening to her talk, the sense of being part of a world that mattered, a teeming world animated by passion and knowledge and belief, a world that he ached to participate in and so wanted intensely to make love to her, not because of his lust or her beauty but because making love to her was his only means of really participating in her life, as if by making love he could become a part of her world.

On his rock above the Saint Lawrence, T jumped upright, startled by a family of sleek, long-necked, furry brown creatures scurrying past his feet. They looked like the offspring of a snake that mated with a duck, and they paused a moment to look at him, yanking him abruptly out of his memories, before hurrying on. He had a sense then of the utter weirdness of time, how it flies and yet never moves, until at his age life sometimes felt, in actuality, like one perpetual, unending moment. Back in Syracuse, then, a heartbeat ago, he had reached across the dining table in the midst of conversation, taken Carolyn's hands in his, and pulled her to him for a kiss. After that, they spent the rest of the afternoon in the bedroom. They went out to a good restaurant for dinner, and then back to her bedroom for the night; the next day he returned to New York for his wedding rehearsal. Then, in another heartbeat, thirty years passed and now Carolyn was dead and he was old and her lively world that he had so desired was lost to him, and he was left alone in his vacuum-sealed world of Salem, Virginia; and now another heartbeat and he was up and putting his shirt on and starting back to the cabin.

Inside, as soon as he closed the door behind him, Jenny called out, "Is that you, T? Lester?" Her voice came from the hallway.

"It's me," he called back. He noticed an orange juice container on the table and poured himself a glass.

"Where's Lester?"

"Still fishing." T finished off the juice and looked out the window, where he could see Lester standing in the boat, reeling in line artfully, with the pole to his side, playing with the action.

"Did you guys catch anything?"

"Nothing," T called back. He put his glass in the sink. "Lester might catch himself a cold, though. He wound up in the water."

"He's a clown," Jenny said. "He's still out there fishing?"

"You can see him from the window. He looks like he's enjoying himself."

"Great," Jenny said. "Come on back here. I'm in the tub."

In the bathroom, he found her submerged from the neck down under a field of bubbles. Her hair was wet and slicked back over her head. "Where," he asked, "did you find bubble-bath?"

"Under the kitchen sink," she said, as if it were absurd to think the cabin might be without bubble-bath. "I was looking for dish detergent."

"Fate," T said.

"Bubbles," she said, then pouted. "But it's lonely in here. I don't have any company."

T sat on the john beside the tub and touched her cheek with the back of his hand. She looked a little pale, and he thought he saw a hint of strain in her eyes. "You want company?"

She leaned into his touch and arched upward slightly as she simultaneously massaged the small of her back, which pushed her body up out of the bubbles. "You could just stare at me," she said. "Or you could get in here with me. That way I wouldn't have to massage my own back." She turned her head quickly and kissed his hand. "You could do it for me."

T went to dry his hands on a long blue towel that was draped over the back of the john. When he picked up the towel, he upset a container of pills underneath it. "What's this?" he asked, holding up the brown plastic vial.

"Tylenol," she said. "Headache." She looked up at him coyly. "Come on in here and make me feel better."

"Jenny," he said, watching her in the bath, where she had tossed her head back and closed her eyes, the white sheet of bubbles sliding down off her breasts and stomach.

"Yes?" she said dreamily. "T?" The wet pink of her skin rose out of the foam of the bath as water dripped from her hair and off her face. She opened her eyes. "Are you getting in with me?" she asked, a touch of indignation now in her tone, as if it were beyond belief that he wouldn't want to get in the bath with her.

T watched her closely for a moment longer, then undressed and got into the tub. He sat behind her with his knees up, leaving her most of the space and water, then slid down as far as he could, so that her head was resting on his chest. He massaged her neck. "Jenny," he said again. He kissed her on the top of her head. "This is crazy," he said, "but . . ." He wrapped his arms around her shoulders and held her tightly.

Jenny purred and reached behind her, between his legs. "What's this I feel?" she said. She seemed a little surprised as she ran her fingers along the hard length of him. "Do baths turn you on?"

T took Jenny by the shoulders and turned her around, so that they were both sitting with their knees up in the tub, facing each other. He slid his legs under her thighs and tried to pull her up onto him, but she resisted, thrusting her arm out and pushing him away. In a moment her expression, which had been coy and seductive all along, turned suddenly sad and then melted into tears. "Jesus," she said. "You're surprising me. I thought . . ."

"What?" he said. "What's wrong? You don't . . . ?"

"I do," she said. "Yes, but—" She covered her face with her hands, mashing clumps of bubbles into her eyes and hair, which she then roughly brushed away with her forearm as she spun around, turning her back to T. "Hold me again," she said. "Please."

T put his arms around her and held her to his chest.

"I can't right now," she said softly. "I'm hurting right now."

"Hurting?" T reached for the pills and saw from the label that they were Tylenol with codeine. "Is it what Lester said?" he asked. "But we didn't—"

"It's just something that happens with me," she said. "It doesn't have to be sex."

T massaged her gently, moving his fingers from her neck to her temples and forehead. "And this has been going on how long?" he asked. "How many years?"

Jenny sank down deeper into the water. "I enjoy sex," she said. "I swear I do. This is just something I have to deal with sometimes." She rubbed his leg under the water, as if to reassure him. "I want to make love to you," she said. "It just can't be right now. It hurts too much."

"Jenny," he said. "With me—" He took her hand and massaged the palm. "I'm concerned," he said, "honestly, with what might cause this kind of thing. It's the medical—"

"I've seen more doctors," she said. "They're all, they have no idea."

"They've checked you out? You've been—"

"I've been to everybody," she said. "I've had every test done." She spoke with her eyes closed. She might have been lying comfortably in her bed talking to a lover. "They're all, they can't find anything. So, I mean, I have at least the consolation of knowing I don't have a tumor or something like that, which, for a long time, I was convinced—"

"But the doctors don't— What kind of pain is it?"

"Do you really need to know this?"

"I don't need to," T said. "I'm concerned for you."

Jenny looked up at him. She seemed to be exploring his face, trying to read it. "Sometimes it's like if I even think about sex. And it always hurts after," she said. "It starts like a dull ache and then it keeps getting deeper until it's like my whole middle is throbbing." With her free hand she played with the surface of the bath water. "But a couple of magic pills and a hot bath fix me right up. And I swear it doesn't hurt during sex. Sex is great. I mean, it can be great. It's just, after—"

T said, "I find it hard to believe— They don't even have any theories, the doctors?"

"They're all," Jenny said, her voice tinged with obvious anger and frustration. "They're all— They don't say, you know: you're crazy. But they're like: it's nothing physical, so— You figure it out. If it's not physical, then what else? Right?"

"But you don't— That's not something—"

"You should feel this—and then tell me it's in my head. Fuck them. That's, you know— That's bullshit."

"All right," T said. He put the hand he'd been massaging back in the water and started in on the other. "Have you tried nontraditional— Other kinds of medicine than traditional, Western—"

"I feel like—" she said. "To me—" She sighed. "Okay," she said, "here comes my fucked-up story. If you get to know me— What's Lester told you?"

"About you? What's he told me about you?"

"I know you didn't talk about fishing all that time. He must have told you something."

"He told me about the trial," T said. "He told me about your uncle."

"Chucky?" She pulled her hand away and slid down a little deeper into the water.

"Both of them, actually," T said. "But mostly the stuff about the pictures and the trial. He said your mother killed your father when she found the pictures."

"That's true," she said, and she arched her neck so that she was looking at him upside down. "How fucked up is that?"

He kissed her on the forehead. "But the pain from sex—" he said. "That goes back before the trial, doesn't it?"

"Goes back forever," she said, and then dropped down into the water until only her eyes were visible above the bubbles.

T said, "Where are you going, Jenny?" and wiped foam away from her hair.

She exhaled into the bubbles, blowing them away, and then emerged and shook her head, splashing water out into the bathroom. "I'll tell you something—he didn't just take pictures of me."

T pulled her back up to his chest. He reached for the towel and wiped water and soap from her face.

"I've always told everybody Chucky only took pictures— *Really, he only took pictures, I swear*—like I was defending him, like he really wasn't that bad, but the truth is—" She turned sideways to look up at him. "I don't know why I want to tell you this."

"Go ahead." He pressed his thumbs into the hollow at the base of her neck and squeezed her shoulders gently. "Go ahead and tell me."

"You know my other uncle, Ronnie," she said, settling herself in the tub again, leaning back to T, "he was the sweetest man on Earth."

"This is the one that drowned himself?"

She nodded. "He was smart, he was gentle, he loved classical guitar— That's his guitar we got with us."

"Lester said."

"Couldn't play worth a shit, though. Always said he was

going to learn soon as he could make the time. Did Lester tell you I was close to him?"

"He did," T said. "He told me that."

"He played backgammon too," she said. "Wasn't particularly good at that either. I started beating him soon as I learned how to play."

"He sounds different from the picture I get of the rest of your family."

"It was mostly that he was sweet," she said. "That's the only word I can think of that describes it. My father was a quiet man too, but weird quiet, like he wasn't really there. Weird that way. You had to know him a while and then you just figured—oh, that's the way he is."

"What was so weird?"

"Just— He wouldn't look at people. He'd watch the ground. He didn't talk, hardly ever. He was weird that way."

"What did he do for a living?"

"Mailman," she said, and laughed. "Figures, doesn't it?"

"And Ronnie?"

"Nothing. Mostly always broke, bumming money from everyone. Worked manual labor for the county when he could."

"And Chucky was the CPA."

"Uncle Chuck," she said. "Chucky's the man with the money. He's the one everybody goes to when they need something. He's generous like that. Gives everybody money, never asks for it back. Takes care of his family, which is what everybody says about him: *Chucky takes care of his family.*"

T moved his thumbs up along her neck into her hairline. He massaged the back of her head.

"I told everyone that Chucky only took pictures. Even during the trial, I couldn't bring myself—even though it might have helped Babs. I still felt this kind of thing with Chuck, like, I couldn't do it. But he didn't only take pictures," she said. "Ever since I can remember, far back as I can remember, he would give me baths. My parents would be around. They were always like, *Chuck's giving the baby her bath* . . . Meanwhile, he'd be sliding his fingers into me. He used to tell me, you need to be clean in there. And then there'd be other things . . . There'd always be some reason, and then the present: a dress, money." She was silent a long while before she turned again to look up at T. "I'm sure he damaged me," she said. "Doctors say they don't see anything physical, but, you know, I feel it. And I know what he used to do, so— That's what I think, fuck what they say. I'm sure he did something to me." She paused a moment and then added, "I always did look forward to the presents, and it's not like, probably always, I didn't know— but I was just a baby." She closed her eyes again, and then was silent.

T continued gently massaging her scalp, and then her forehead and temples. Through the uncurtained and ornately framed window above the tub, sunlight came into the bathroom and cast a pinkish-orange hue against the walls and down into the corners, where dust gathered. From the light, he guessed it was late afternoon. He could smell the wood smoke from the bedroom fireplace, even there in the humid air of the bath, with the softness of Jenny's body against his chest and the hard porcelain of the tub against his back. The bath water had cooled to tepid, and he considered for a moment offering to heat up another pail, but then realized he didn't want to get out of the tub. He didn't want to let go of Jenny, whom he was holding now with his arms around her and his hands clasped over her stomach.

In the bath with Jenny, her body willing under his touch, it was easy to forget the last few years, which were coming quickly to feel like a darkness, a shadow behind him. He held her head in his hands and ran the tips of his fingers over her mouth and nose and eyes. She had drifted off into a peaceful stillness, from which she stirred slightly. When he kissed the back of her head and pressed his lips into her hair, she said, "You're very intense, you know that?"

"Me?" he said. "I'm moved— By what you told me."

She was quiet a moment and then asked, "Could you be with someone— Someone with my kind of problems, my kind of history?"

"What do you mean by *be with*, Jenny? You can't get much more *with* someone then we are at the moment."

"We're not with each other at all," she said. "We're just messing around; we're just passing through."

"This is getting too cryptic for me."

"It's not cryptic. Could you ever have a relationship with someone like me, a serious relationship?"

"If I weren't more than thirty years older than you," he said, "there wouldn't be any problem. No problem at all."

"You're hung up on the age thing." She took his hands in hers and wrapped them around her tightly. "I feel a connection with you. I don't know that I've ever felt anything like it before, to be honest." She pushed her body back into his and covered her breasts with his hands. "Plus," she looked up at him mischievously, "you're rich. What else could a girl want?"

"Youth," T said. "The possibility of sharing a full life with someone."

"I'll take any life I can get," she fired back. "This idiotic mess I was born to—really," she said.

T pulled the bath plug. "Water's getting cold. How are you feeling?"

"Better." She toyed with the bubbles. "You make me better."

T got out of the tub, found a dry towel, and held it up for her.

"Ooh," she said. "Just like royalty."

"Lester," he said, drying her shoulders and back, "Lester's negotiating for sixty grand."

"Sixty?" She turned to face him. "He only stole forty. I told you that. He's asking you to give him sixty thousand?"

"You didn't know he'd ask for sixty?" T said. "I thought you might have discussed it before we went fishing."

"No," she said. "We didn't talk about that. Did he say why he wanted that much?"

"He says you both could use the extra to get yourself settled after you pay off this Short Willie character." He patted the towel between her breasts. "Is that really the guy's name?"

"Really," she said. "Lester does have a point. Those assholes did ten thousand worth of damage to my house, easy." She took a towel from the sink and began to dry T's back as he bent over to dry her stomach and thighs. "Can you afford that much?" she asked. "Is that possible?"

"I'm thinking about it."

"But can you afford it?" she pressed. "Can you get your hands on that much cash?"

"That's not a problem."

"Really? How? How do you do something like that, just come up with that much cash?"

"I can arrange a bank wire," he said. "All we need to do is find the local bank. It's not a problem."

"What a different world you live in." She kissed him, a peck on the lips. *"Not a problem,"* she said. "Sixty thousand dollars."

Between the fire and the heat of the afternoon, the bedroom felt like a sauna, and T went immediately to the windows, which he opened top and bottom. He joined Jenny where she had thrown herself onto the bed. They lay naked a while side by side, holding hands, each staring at the ceiling, before Jenny turned to cuddle closer to him. "God," she said, "I'm so comfortable with you."

T rested the palm of his hand on the base of her spine, his fingers reaching to the softer flesh. He said, "Let's say we went to the bank Monday morning and I arranged for the money. Would you want to go back to Chattanooga then, with Lester and the cash?"

"I guess," she said. "I guess I'd have to. No way I'd trust him to make the arrangements by himself."

"What arrangements?"

"He can't just walk up to Short Willie with a bag full of money. They'd kill him and take the money, and then— I don't know where I'd stand then."

"So what kind of arrangements?" T asked again.

"We'd have to find a middleman to make a deal. I don't know what Willie's going to want. Anything's possible with him. He might say, Okay, I won't kill you, but you've got to give me fifty thousand and leave the country. Or, Give me the money back, along with your right hand."

"Your right hand?"

"Believe me, T. This guy is so fucked up. I'm terrified of him. He's capable of absolutely anything."

"Your right hand," T repeated. "Really?"

"Or worse. He might want his balls. With Willie, like I said—"

"Okay," T said. "So, how would you get back to Chattanooga? What were you thinking?"

"We could take the Rover," she said, her hand casually moving over his sex, cupping it before following a line of hair up his stomach. "You could wait for me here. After we give the money back, I could make arrangements to have my house taken care of, and then I could come back for you. We could probably do the whole thing in three or four days."

"And then what?" T said. "After you're back here. Then what?"

"I don't know," she said. "It's an adventure. What did you have in mind?" She climbed on top of him, lining up her legs and torso with his so that no part of her touched the bed. "A guy my own age," she said, grinning, "they'd be pinning me down and raping me by now, I tried to stop them. They wouldn't give a damn. But an older guy like you— You have control. I get to play with you," she said, pressing her breasts against his chest and kissing him on the lips. "This is nice," she continued. "We can cuddle and touch and I don't have to, you know. I mean, not every time, we don't absolutely have to do the wild thing."

"The wild thing," T said, repeating Jenny thoughtlessly. He stroked her hair and drops of water fell onto his chest. "Have you ever been to Crete?" he asked.

"Where's that?"

"Greece," he said. "Off the tip of Greece."

Jenny laughed. "I went to New York City once when I was a little girl. We went to the top of the World Trade Center. Mostly though I haven't left the South."

"Crete's beautiful," he said. "I have a villa there. It's a cottage, really—but I call it my villa. I could take you to Crete and be the envy of all the Greek men."

"Because of me?" she said coyly.

"You know because of you."

"You really have a house there? Who takes care of it?"

"A local couple," he said.

"Do you go a lot?"

"Used to," T said. He was about to say *before the arrest*, but caught himself in time. "I haven't been in a few years now. Do you think you'd like something like that? Living in Crete for a while?"

She kissed him on the lips. "It sounds like a dream." She rolled off him and snuggled into his side, her head against his neck. "It sounds like a fantasy, something that couldn't possibly come true."

"All you'd have to do is come back and get me," T said, after a second, his eyes on the ceiling. "We could fly from here. Just . . . go."

"*You're* like a dream," Jenny said. "Tell me more things we could do."

"Actually," T said, "we'd have to get you a passport first. And I'd have to go pick up mine in Salem."

"Salem?"

"Virginia. Where I have a house. Where I've been living."

T felt Jenny nod, and when he turned to look at her he saw that she was falling asleep. He pulled a sheet up from the foot of the bed and draped it over their midsections, leaving feet and torsos exposed. "Jenny?" he said.

"Um, hmm."

"Remember the older woman I told you about? The one I had an affair with when I was your age?"

"Um-hmm."

"She would never tell me her age, but I guessed she was forty-one, and I used to do this counting thing where I'd tell myself: when I'm thirty-one, she'll be fifty-one; when I'm forty-one, she'll be sixty-one."

Jenny laughed, a small, quiet laugh.

"Have you done that?" he asked. "With me?"

She shook her head.

"When you're thirty-three," he said. "I'll be sixty-seven. When you're forty-three, I'll be seventy-seven—if I'm lucky. Males in my family generally don't make it past seventy-five. My father died at sixty-six."

"T," she said softly, in a whisper, "right now I'm just trying to get to tomorrow."

"You'll get there," he said. "I promise. I give you my word."

Jenny nuzzled into him closer. "You'll do it, then?" she whispered. "You've decided? You'll get us the money?"

He nodded. "I'll do it for you."

She kissed him on the neck. "I'm so sleepy," she said. "Hold me. Take a nap with me."

T pulled the sheet over their shoulders and held Jenny in his arms. From outside, beyond the window, came the chatter of squirrels and then the coughing sound of a small engine being pull-started and then the growl of the engine as it caught and Lester, he assumed, revved it a few times before dropping the prop into the water, signaled by a change in tone, a deepening, before it began to move away, the sound eventually diminishing to silence.

. 3 .

T lay in bed looking up at Lester, who stood over him pointing a gun at his head. He had awakened to Lester tapping the barrel of the gun gently but persistently against his forehead, as if knocking softly on a closed door. He had awakened calmly and fully, with a sense of simply appearing in a dark room in the middle of a scene. First he wasn't there. Then he was. Their eyes met and for several seconds they stared at each other in silence. Jenny cuddled alongside T, spooning him, her arm around his chest, her cheek against the back of his neck, her breath shallow and soft. There wasn't as much as a glow left in the embers of the fireplace, but still the wood-smoke odor filled the bedroom, and the wind, which had picked up again, hummed in the chimney. What light there was in the room, the light in which T watched Lester's expression, came from outside, through the open window, from the bright fields of stars and an orange moon that hovered low and full on the horizon.

The gun in Lester's hand was small and black, maybe six or seven inches long from the hammer, which was cocked, to the barrel, which floated a foot away from T's head, aimed at the bridge of his nose. It was a sleek, attractive weapon, with a silvery trigger curved like a crescent moon inside the black circle of the trigger guard. Lester's thumb rested on the hammer. His fingers were wrapped around the butt of the gun, one finger looped through the trigger guard, behind the trigger. T lifted his head and rested it comfortably in the palm of his hand, his elbow pressed into the pillow—a gesture meant to prompt an explanation from Lester, as if to say, *Well? What next?* Lester let the gun drop to his side. His eyes moved from T to Jenny. They followed the length of her body, from the spill of her hair over the pillow, down her bare shoulders and back, and along her thighs and legs to her feet. He seemed to swallow her with his eyes. His face softened and his mouth opened just slightly as if to release a small, silent moan. Then he looked again at T, tucked the gun into the waistband of his pants, and left the room without a word.

T settled his head down again in the pillow and pushed his body back into the warmth of Jenny's body. Part of him thought it might be a good idea simply to go back to sleep, though the further he traveled toward wakefulness the more concerned he became about Lester pointing a gun at his head. He had been in the midst of a dream when Lester so disturbingly called him back to the world. In the dream he had been right where he really was, lying next to Jenny in bed, and he had actually thought he was awake—but now he remembered a moment in which a crowd of strangers had gathered around the bed and he had walked away from them and wandered into an abandoned house, a destroyed place that had once been beautifully appointed with furniture and art but now was a hodgepodge of rubble, everything battered and broken and smashed. He wandered uneasily through the house, sad at the loss, and then he was aware, with a growing sense of terror, of a presence, a force, and all he knew for sure was that the force or presence was ominous and that it was responsible for the destruction and that if he didn't get out of the house, it would destroy him too. Then a couple of things happened quickly. First, in looking for an exit, he had come upon a room with a little boy in it, a boy barely a toddler, who was frightened, and in the dream T was unable to comfort him. Then Jenny walked into the room and picked up the child and carried him out of the house, with T following. The dream left him wonderfully calm—which was why, he guessed, he had reacted with such composure to the sight of Lester standing over him with a gun.

That he had dreamed anything at all surprised him, given he had stopped dreaming since leaving New York—or at least he had stopped remembering his dreams. When he was young, he used to have nightmares all the time, so much so that for a while around age nine or ten he had been afraid to go to bed at night. He'd dream of terrifying monsters in the bedroom, demons behind walls. In what he'd since decided must have been a regular if temporary psychotic state that came about when fear awakened him just enough to keep him suspended midway between sleep and dream, he'd hear the heavy-footed approach of monsters as clearly as birdsong in the morning and equally real. When he'd try to scream, he'd produce a dry rasp. His father, a naturally cold man with little interest in his son, didn't want to hear about it. Once he carried T crying up the stairs to his room and literally threw him down onto his bed. He told him to be a man, then turned out the lights and slammed the door as he left. His mother took him to see Father Cardinale, who told him to pray to Jesus before going to sleep each night and ask him to take away the dreams. He did. Jesus didn't. The lucid dreams persisted on and off through his twenties. Once, in college, he awoke crawling across his dorm-room carpet, trying to escape something. Once, spending the night with Carolyn at her house, he'd leaped from her bed and stumbled out of her bedroom before finally awakening in a dark hall.

Eventually the power of the dreams diminished until, all the years with Alicia, he had dreamed rarely, and the last year in Salem, he hadn't dreamed at all. When his daughter, Maura, turned out to have the same problem, he'd understood that it was simply something built into his nature and not a matter of having an uncaring father or an ineffectual mother. Maura had the same horrid dreams, perhaps even more intensely since she complained of waking hallucinations, of seeing things in the corners of her vision that she knew weren't there. Once she told him she had lain in bed for a half hour in the morning listening to a lovely piano concerto, only to realize on her way to the shower that it had all been in her head. She had heard it, she said, with absolute clarity. Neither he nor Maura was crazy, but they both, in their youth at least, had violent minds, violent in that they threatened to break through the boundaries between what was real and what wasn't. Maura subjugated hers with a regimen of study and extracurricular activities that kept her intensely busy every waking minute of her young life. He understood this. A disorderly mind required an orderly world to keep it in check. He hadn't figured out a similar tack until much later in life, when he discovered the world of business.

Jenny had been beautiful in his dream. She had entered the room of the crying child like a vision. He couldn't remember what she was wearing. Her hair was long and flowing. She was so beautiful that just looking at her did something tangible to him, produced within him something he could feel, a sense of longing that was physical, as if to touch her would be the fulfillment of all his desires. Even as he lay in bed worrying more and more about Lester, he could almost feel the dream again. He could almost recall that sense of yearning at the sight of Jenny. Once, in his early teens, after being awakened by a nightmare, he had wandered out into his back yard, where he had seen a single light on in his neighbor's otherwise dark house. Without thinking much about what he was doing, he stealthily climbed a trellis to peek into the lighted room through the inch or two of space between the bottom of a shade and the window sill. Inside the room, his neighbor's daughter, a girl a year ahead of him in school, was standing in front of a full-length mirror in her bedroom, inspecting and taking measure of her body, her pajamas on the floor at her feet. She'd pull her shoulders up and look at her breasts with her head cocked to the side. She'd turn her back to the mirror and twist her head around to see how she looked from behind. She did this for several minutes before lazily pulling her pajama bottoms back on and buttoning up her top while she gazed dreamily at nothing. When she turned off the light and disappeared in blackness, he climbed down quietly from the trellis and went back into his own yard, where he lay a long while on the grass with his eyes closed, trying to recall her every movement in front of the mirror. For the rest of his life, he'd remember those few minutes, and he'd never really understand why, except that, like Jenny in his dream, the beauty of his neighbor's body and the stolen intimacy of watching her unobserved seemed somehow to transport him to a place so much more desirable than the revealed, ordinary world.

T considered waking Jenny and decided against it. He rubbed his eyes, wiping away the last vestiges of sleep, and pulled himself up in bed. From the kitchen, he heard the rush of running water in the sink followed by a high-pitched moan from the water pipes, then a moment of silence after the last squeak of the old-fashioned faucet, then a heavy crash that was the sound of a water glass falling to the floor and breaking, and finally a soft curse and footsteps into the living room and the sound of a body dropping down into the cushions of the couch with a moan. He stood in the moonlit bedroom and went quietly as he could manage to his suitcase, where he found fresh clothes neatly folded and arranged. As he pulled on his underwear, careful not to make a sound, and slipped into khaki slacks and a blue knit shirt, he practically leaned out into the hallway listening to the various small sounds, the clanks and knocks, coming from the living room. He again considered waking Jenny as he sat on the edge of the bed to put on his shoes and socks, and again decided against it. He hesitated a moment longer, his heart beating fast and hard, then stood and went out into the hallway with all the casual bravado he could manage.

Lester was on the couch in a long tongue of moonlight from the cabin's front windows. He was sitting up, leaning forward with his weight on the balls of his feet, his elbows on his knees, holding his head in his hands. He seemed not to be aware of T. He sat on the couch breathing hard, the heels of his feet tapping a rapid beat against the air. He was barefoot and shirtless, the top button of his jeans undone and the zipper down an inch. The guitar case was opened at the foot of the couch and the guitar lay on the cushions next to his thigh. The instrument, as Lester had promised, was red. It was, however, an unusual shade of red, a resonant terra-cotta, an earthy red that brought to mind wet clay or a vein of muted crimson inside a rock crystal. The wood's texture and polish was lustrous, the fingerboard inlaid with a naturally dark wood and spaced with silvery frets. As T watched from the hallway, taking in the scene, the guitar seemed to glow in the moonlight. It seemed to vibrate slightly, as if it might at any second simply rise up and float out the window, following the trail of moonlight off into darkness.

In the center of the kitchen, a puddle of water was spiked with shards of broken glass. T sat on the arm of the couch. Lester nodded several times, more jerking his head than nodding. He seemed to be acknowledging T's presence, though his face remained buried in his hands and his feet kept tapping their manic rhythm. T touched the guitar, running a single finger along the edge of the neck. He noticed, through the sound hole, a sliver of crumpled aluminum foil inside the guitar. Next to it lay a length of blue rubber tubing, maybe an eighth of an inch in diameter. He plucked the low E string with his thumb. It made a sick, wobbly sound.

"Don't do that," Lester said through his hands. "Fuck's wrong with you? Fucking asshole. Fucking clown. Fucking old man." He rocked back and forth as he spoke each curse.

"Lester—"

"Don't fucking Lester." He took his hands away from his face and looked at T for the first time. "You piece of shit. You arrogant sum' bitch."

T said, "Look—"

"Don't fuckin' look nothing." He jammed his hand through the sound hole into the guitar box and came up with the gun. He cocked the hammer and pointed it at T's head.

"This again?" T said, again surprising himself with his calm.

"I'm thinking maybe I should blow you away. I'm thinking maybe you should die, T. What do you think?"

T said, "What the hell happened, Lester? I thought we had—"

"Shut up," he said through his teeth. "Shut up, you miserable fuck."

"I'll shut up," T said. "But can you tell me—"

Lester shoved the barrel of the gun into T's chest, nearly knocking him off the arm of the couch. He said, "You don't sound like you shutting up."

T steadied himself and crossed his arms over his chest.

"That's better," Lester said. "You know what? You're scum. I know you think it's me, it's *us*—but know what? That ain't way it is." He paused a moment and looked T up and down, almost as if he had suddenly forgot who he was talking to. He blinked and rubbed his eyes. He asked T, "Who you think I am?"

T said, "What do you mean, Lester? What do you mean, who do I think you are?"

"I mean what's my fucking last name, Tom, 'T' Walker? Tom 'T' *Aloysius* Walker? You got four fuckin' names, how come I only got one? That all you think I'm worth? One name?"

"It never came up," T said. "I don't know. What's your last name?"

Lester tapped the side of the gun against his heart several times, hard, a gesture that mystified T. Trying to read the gesture felt like trying to interpret a foreign language. T folded his hands in his lap, half paralyzed with calm. He looked like a counselor working with an hysterical patient, trying to calm him with his own calm. He sat on the armrest, an older man neatly dressed in khaki slacks and a knit shirt, looking across the moonlit cushions at a shirtless, long-haired youth in unbuttoned jeans holding a small, lethal-looking pistol in his hand.

"Deveraux," Lester said. "Got some French, got some Cherokee." He rubbed the butt of the gun against his temple as if trying to relieve a sudden itch. "You think I'm the scum," he said, with his eyes closed. "But ain't me," he said. "Ain't Jenny."

T said, "I don't think anybody's scum."

Lester nodded but didn't respond.

"Lester," T said, "can you tell me what's going on? I thought—"

"Shut the fuck up, T." He leaned back and held the gun in his lap with both hands. "I'm celebrating," he said. "You got a problem with me celebrating?"

"No problem," T said. "What are you celebrating?"

"Fish." He smiled, as if suddenly pleased. "Caught me a stringer of fish. Man," he said, excited, "soon as it got dark, bro— Fish started hittin' like fuck-what, man. Boom, boom, boom," he punched the air. "One after 'nother. Got must be fuckin' eight fish out there on the stringer. Swear God."

"No kidding," T said. "What kind?"

Lester gave T a sideways grin. He said, "You interested, huh?"

"Sure," T said. "What did you catch?"

"You mean while I was out there fishin' and you was in here with Jenny?"

"Yes," T said. "What did you get?"

"Pickerel, I think, mostly. One monster: fuckin' huge, must be three feet long, swear God."

"Brown?" T said. "Sharp teeth, like the pickerel?"

"Uh-huh," Lester said, watching T carefully, the gun still in his lap.

"Sounds like a northern pike."

Lester nodded solemnly. "So how come you fuckin' her again after I told you—" He grimaced, as if suddenly in pain. "*I told you* how much it hurt her and you in there at it again."

"We didn't—"

"Shut the fuck up, *we*." Lester sat up straight, holding a cushion with his left hand, his right hand on the gun. "*We,*" he repeated. "What do you think, *we*? What are you like, high school romance now? You fuckin' asshole."

"Nobody's—"

"Thing is," Lester said, pointing the gun at T, more gesture than threat, "onliest thing is, you know you hurtin' her. That's the only thing far as I'm concerned. She's about money, can't blame her. She need money to get out. You got the money. That's way it is for her. But you, you piece of shit. You think we're scum? You hurtin' her like that?"

"I'm not hurting her."

"Fuck you're not," Lester said quietly. "You know you are." He paused a second and then repeated himself even more quietly. "You know you are."

"Are you high?" T asked. "I don't get the sudden change, Lester. A few hours ago, you were making a deal with me. Now—"

Lester interrupted as if he hadn't heard a word T said. "I never known Jenny to be with a guy much as she's bein' with you. You know what I'm sayin'?"

"No," T said, "I don't."

"What's she sayin' to you, man? She sayin' that she loves you? She tellin' you that shit?"

"Lester—"

"She is, isn't she? Fuckin' bitch. You believe her?"

"Look, Lester—" T touched his forehead, as if it might help him stay focused. "Can you answer my one question, please?" he said. "Didn't we have a deal? What happened?"

"She lying to you." He leaned forward again, dropping back into his original position, holding his face in his hands, only now there was a gun in his right hand, the butt of it against his eye. "My daddy," he said, "he basically a decent man. All he really care about, 'course, was fishing and fuck-ing—and didn't really matter who he did either with. He basically a good man, though."

"I'm sure he was," T said.

"You sure he was," Lester mocked. "Get the fuck out of here," he hissed. "Swear God I'm inch away from puttin' a bullet through one of your eyes."

T stood. "I don't get it," he said.

"You two seconds from being dead, you don't get the fuck out of here."

T backed away several steps, then turned and walked down the hall to the bedroom. Inside, he closed the door behind him gently, careful to make as little noise as possible. Under his breath, he cursed the lack of a lock on the bedroom door, then scanned the room for a chair he might wedge under the knob—though he knew there was no such chair in the room. Behind him, Jenny lay on her side wrapped in a sheet and clutching a pillow to her breast. His heart was beating hard enough that he could feel it through his shirt, and he placed the palm of his hand over it and rubbed, as if trying to massage it to a regular beat. He sat on the edge of the bed, by Jenny's feet, and waited in the dark for his breathing to even out and his heart to slow down. When he woke Jenny in a moment to tell her what was going on, he didn't want to sound breathless and scared.

T didn't know much about violence. Once, at the gaming tables in Las Vegas, he had seen a man attack a dealer. He had gone with Brooke to Vegas, and at one point in the trip, he had been playing blackjack when the player next to him grabbed the dealer by her throat and pulled her over all the other players, scattering their cards and chips. The dealer was a strikingly beautiful woman in her twenties, with short dark hair, and he had thrown her to the ground, ripped her blouse half off, and punched her in the face multiple times before security finally gave up on trying to wrestle him off her and simply knocked him unconscious with a series of blows to the head using some kind of weapon T couldn't quite make out, something small and lethal. The dealer had lost her shoes when he dragged her over the table, and she stood up, barefoot, with her blouse ripped open and her bra down around her stomach, and pushed people away from her—the people trying to attend to her—and went back to her station to resume her dealing position. She had already picked up a deck and was feeding it into an automatic shuffler before people realized she was in shock and forcibly covered her up and carried her away as she screamed curses for them to leave her alone and put her down. Within minutes, two minutes, three at the most, everything was back to normal; everything was exactly as it had been: dealers dealing, players playing, pit crew doing what they do. The whole violent incident was like a momentary disturbance in a fast-moving river.

But T had never forgotten what it felt like to be right there next to that woman when she was attacked. It was as if the ordinary world were suddenly ripped away, something red and huge exploding out of a hidden place to pull her over the table and onto the floor. Almost impossible to explain how the very fabric of the world seemed to rip as the man's heavy fists crashed down on her face, bloodying her lip and nose. When he pulled off her clothes, it was as if he were trying to tear through her skin. Later, T used words like *savage* and *vicious* to describe the attack, but there was no way, really, to get across how the world seemed to melt away under his feet, how everything felt suddenly changed and violated.

When he rubbed Jenny's shoulder, she opened her eyes, turned her head slightly to look up at him, and then closed her eyes again as if settling back into sleep.

"Jenny," he whispered, "you need to wake up." He patted her hair and kissed her on the cheek. "Jen," he said.

"What?" she pushed her head down deeper into the pillow, her voice husky with sleep.

"Lester's got a gun," he said. "He was pointing it at us; pointing it at me."

She turned over onto her back and crossed her arms under her head. She seemed immediately awake. "Lester pointed a gun at you?"

"Did you know he had a gun?"

She nodded. "A little one. A .38. He pointed it at you?"

"He's acting completely different," T said. "I think he might be high."

"What do you mean *completely different?*"

"I mean he's like a different person. He doesn't even sound the same. Now he's got this country-Southern accent he didn't have before."

"Fuck," Jenny said and closed her eyes. She added, "The shit's country to the bone. Comes out when he's wrecked. He can't hide it."

"What's going on?" T asked. "Is he dangerous?"

"Fucking jerk," she said. "He didn't have his works out, did he? Please don't tell me he had his works out."

"What are works?"

"Needle, spoon—haven't you ever even seen a movie of somebody shooting up?"

"I didn't see a needle or any of that," T said. "I did see a blue rubber thing, like they wrap around their arms."

"Just that?" Jenny asked.

"It was inside the guitar. I saw it through the hole."

"I don't know," Jenny said. "It doesn't sound like he shot up."

"He shoots up? What, crank?"

"Every once in a blue moon. He won't mess around with that shit but, you know, maybe a few times a year."

T climbed onto the bed and sat up next to Jenny. "He's crazy. What the hell are we supposed to do?"

"Ride it out," she said. She put her head on his thigh. "Just stay away from him till morning."

T stroked her hair. Lester was quiet in the living room. The only sounds were gusts of wind in the trees and rattling cabin windows. He relaxed against the headboard and shifted his weight to get comfortable. Jenny wrapped herself around him, holding on as if he were a blanket or a talisman that made her feel more secure. He closed his eyes and tried to settle in for the night. He thought, how different this moment in the Thousand Islands with Jenny and all those other moments half a lifetime ago with Carolyn. Now it was Jenny clinging to him as if he might keep her afloat through this night, and back then he had been the one clinging. He ran his hand along Jenny's shoulder and over her arm, feeling tender toward her, for a moment seeing himself in her, remembering that feeling that someone else was in control and all you had to do was hold on and they'd take you with them along the right path, the safe way, the good way. But Carolyn had taken him nowhere. Her train stopped at the awarding of his degree, and once on his own he rambled as if lost for many years after. About that Alicia had been right. He had thought a great deal about what she said for a long time after she said it: he'd drifted for years until he married Brooke. Brooke gave him Maura and work and a path to follow, and he'd married Alicia to keep him on course. As he stroked Jenny's arm in the wood-smoke-scented air of the bedroom, his thoughts rushed along the whole course of his life, as if in those few moments in the dark bedroom he might be able somehow to make sense of it, the life road he'd followed, the path that took him from a childhood on Long Island, to college in Syracuse, to a love affair with his professor, to years of wandering, to Brooke and marriage and Maura and a life in business, to abandonment by Brooke, as he had been abandoned by Carolyn, to Alicia and Evan and a few good years of their blended family, and then abandonment by Alicia, and he'd honestly never before that moment in bed with Jenny seen it that way, that every woman he loved abandoned him, and it hit him with enough power to make his body stiffen as he asked the obvious question, which was why that should be so—and when he had no answer, he let it go, and continued following his journey which led him after Alicia to Salem, and from there to here, back in the Thousand Islands, where he lay in bed with Jenny Cross, a Southern girl born into squalor and abuse and on the run from drug dealers, and outside beyond the closed bedroom door Lester high and brandishing a pistol, and T in a silent few moments casting the net of his thoughts over all of it as if there were an answer somewhere to find, and then the disturbing notion shot through him like a premonition that he needed to figure it out, to put his story together, this instant, this moment, this night.

"I'm sorry," T said. He'd heard Jenny ask a question, but the words hadn't registered. "What was that?"

"Did you say he pointed the gun at *us?*" Jenny asked. She looked up at him, her head still resting on his thigh. "Before? Is that what you said?"

"He was in here while we were sleeping," T said. "I woke up and he was pointing it at my head."

"But not me?"

"No," T said. "He pointed it at me. At least that's all I saw."

Jenny put her arms around T's waist and snuggled up comfortably, as if she were ready to go back to sleep. "He probably popped some shit and got himself totally fucked up," she said. "He'll be all right in the morning."

"I've got a bad feeling. I'm nervous about all this."

Jenny put a hand on his knee and kissed his thigh. "Guy just pointed a loaded gun at your head," she said. "Only natural you'd have a bad feeling."

"You think that's it?"

"Sure it is," she said, and the instant she said it, Lester kicked the bedroom door open and then stood there in the hallway.

Jenny grabbed T around the chest, as if trying to jump into him. "What the fuck are you doing?" she yelled at Lester. "You scared the shit out of me!"

Lester grinned. His hair was pushed back roughly off his forehead and tucked behind his ears, as if he'd been trying to keep it off his face. The pistol was tucked down into the elastic band of his underwear, which showed through the half-open zipper of his jeans. He folded his hands over his chest, and the muscles in his shoulders and arms stood out dramatically in the moonlight. His eyes were dark and wild. His face was tight: the rectangle of it, the squarish chin and flattened plane of mouth, eyes, and nose, looked as though it might have been carved out of weathered stone. "I sneaked up," he said softly. "I was hoping to hear you two getting down."

"Lester," Jenny said.

Lester said, "How many times you doing this guy, Jenny? Till it kills you? What up with that?"

Jenny said, "You're spun. Look at you."

Lester's grin changed into a mischievous smile.

"You're going to blow this whole thing," she said, her tone of voice shifting unmistakably into intimacy with him.

Lester said, "You a piece of work, Jenny Cross." He stared at her a long moment, the smile disappearing along with the mischievousness, and then he walked away, his footsteps traveling down the hall and out the front door.

T said, "What 'whole thing'? What was that about?"

Jenny climbed over T, out of the bed, and put on the sundress Lester had bought for her. She wrapped it around her, tying the belt savagely with a knot. "Fuck," she said. "He's spun. He's out of control. I don't know what the hell he's doing."

"But what was that about?" T said, standing in front of her. "What 'whole thing' were you talking about?"

"Look," Jenny said. She put her hands on T's waist. "Far as Lester knows, we're scamming you. We get the cash, and then we take off."

"And not come back for me?" T said. "You're conning me out of the money?"

"Far as Lester knows, that's the story. I'm just playing you so I can get him the money."

"But it's not really—"

"No. Jesus," she said. She pressed her body into his, wrapping her arms around him tightly. "Can't you tell?" she said. "Don't you know?"

T didn't answer for a moment. Then he wrapped his arms around her and held the back of her head in his hand. "Okay," he said. "All right."

When she pulled away from him, her eyes were wet, and he wiped them gently with the back of his hand. "The story you've told me," he asked, "is that true, about this Willie character and the drugs?"

"It's all true," she said. "I swear to God."

"So what is this about with Lester?" he asked. "What's he doing?"

"He's crazy like this," she said, and covered her eyes with her hands for a moment, as if trying to think. "He's just— There's no dealing with him." Then she looked to T as if hoping he might know what to do.

T took a second to think, then went out to the hall bathroom with Jenny following behind. He found his pants on the back of the john. The pockets were empty, front and back.

Jenny said, "He's got your keys?"

"And wallet," T said. As he said it, the front door of the cabin banged open, and then Lester was standing in the bathroom doorway.

"What the fuck you guys doing in here?" Lester put his hand over his heart, as if shocked to find Jenny and T together in the bathroom.

T held up his pants. "Lookin' for my wallet," he said.

"What you need your wallet for, Tom?" When T didn't answer, Lester took a step into the bathroom as he pulled out the pistol and then let it dangle at his side. "I said what you need your wallet for?" His breathing was suddenly slower and deeper.

The bathroom was small and dark, with only the faintest moonlight glowing through a window over the tub. Jenny leaned against the wall with her feet spread and her fingers looped through the belt of her sundress. T turned to her, and it occurred to him that she looked like a cowgirl with her wild head of blond hair and her fingers in her belt. It was an odd thought, given the situation—but he knew he wasn't about to come up with a response for Lester. Whatever words he might have ever had were jammed down in his belly somewhere at the sight of the gun in Lester's hand and even more at the tone of Lester's voice and the look about him as he took that step into the bathroom.

Jenny said, as if amused, "Lester? Isn't this like some kind of bad dream, the three of us cramped up in a dark little room like this?"

Lester said, "Why you doing me this way, Jenny?"

Jenny said, "What are you talking about? Lester? What are you thinking?"

Lester didn't answer. He appeared disappointed in Jenny. He appeared saddened by her.

"Can we go outside?" she said. "Can you and I talk a minute?"

"No," he said. "Ain't no fuckin' reason for that anymore."

She leaned toward him and crossed her arms over her chest in a gesture of mock bravado, as if she wanted to be aggressive but was obviously scared. "What's going on?" she said. "What's that mean, no reason?"

"Mean ain't no reason."

"Why not?" she asked, as if straining to understand him. "Why not?" she repeated. "What's changed?"

"You changed," he said. "You think I don't know you, Jenny? You think I don't know you inside out?"

"For God's sake," she said, exasperated. "How high'd you get, Les? How fuckin' cranked are you?"

"Cranked," he said, and he looked behind him, at a plastic wastebasket in the corner. He turned it over and sat down on it. "Don't mean I ain't got you nailed down. You think I don't know what the fuck you doing, Jenny?"

"Just crank?" Jenny said. "That all? 'Cause you really—"

"I don't know," Lester said. "I'm got a bunch of shit going on."

"You got a bunch of shit going on," Jenny echoed. "What's that mean? Did you cook—"

"Oh, shut the fuck up, will you, Jen?" Lester looked to T. "You even think you know what you trying to get yourself into here, T? You even think you got a clue who this girl is?"

"All I know—" T said, finding his voice, surprised at how solid it sounded, "all I know is that I thought we had a deal."

"Yeah, we had a deal," Lester said. "But you want to know?" he added, as if about to reveal something important. "I'll tell you," he said. "It's all where you stand. It's all where you stand at any moment. You see? You see what I'm saying?"

Jenny said, "You're wrecked, Lester. You're not making sense."

"I'm making sense," Lester said. "You just ain't gettin' it." He pointed the gun at T. "You gettin' it?" he asked.

T said, "I wish you wouldn't point that thing at me."

Lester ignored him. "Deal was Jenny for sixty grand," he said. "Bottom line. Right?" When T didn't answer, he repeated himself: "I said, *right?*"

T shook his head. He didn't seem to be fully in control of his actions. "No," he said, and could hardly believe the word had come out of his mouth. It was clearly not what Lester wanted to hear.

"What'd you think the deal?" he asked.

"I give you the money," T said, "to get your lives straightened out. After that Jenny'd be free to make whatever choice she wanted."

"You a fool, you really think that," Lester said. "You'll pay sixty so Jenny can choose? I don't think so. I think you making a buy and you know it."

"I don't think I'm a fool," T said.

"Lester," Jenny said. "Is it registering, what he just told you?" She spoke loudly and articulated each word, as if desperate to get through to him. "He's going to give us sixty thousand dollars. We can pay off Willie—and we'll still have twenty left. Do you get that? Do you hear what he's saying?"

Lester smiled broadly. "I'm spun," he said. "I ain't deaf, and I ain't dumb."

"Then what are you doing? What are you doing, Les?"

Lester held the butt of the gun against his forehead, as if the cool metal were helping relieve a headache. "What I'm doing is fuck the money," he said. He looked up at Jenny sadly. "I'm a dead man, Jen. You know that. It ain't like you don't know it. Willie kills me and you take the extra twenty and come back to your sugar daddy. You know that how it plays out we go back there. All I'm doing going back is getting you off the hook—and only reason he won't kill you is because Chuck. He killin' me, why should I give his money back first? You think I'm stupid? You think I don't know what you're doing?"

Jenny said, "I don't think you're stupid. I think you're out of it."

"I'm not out of it," he said. "I'm deep into it. I'm inside it,

Jenny. I see it perfect clear." He stood up, pointed the gun at T's heart, and pulled the trigger.

T jumped as the gun went off, the explosion resounding like a car backfiring. The bullet hit him just under the collarbone. It felt like being punched hard in the shoulder, and was followed by a surprisingly minimal amount of pain. It felt like what he'd imagine being stabbed would feel like: heat, intense heat on the surface of the wound, rawness, instant radical soreness, and burning—but inside only a dull sickness and not that much pain. The bullet knocked him into the tub and he fell over the porcelain lip, landing comically with his feet sticking up. Falling, he had struck the back of his head on something, and his neck hurt more than the bullet wound. His neck felt like it was broken, and the first thing he did, lying in the bathtub with a bullet in his chest, was wiggle his toes to make sure he wasn't paralyzed.

Jenny appeared at the edge of the tub, followed by Lester. She looked down blankly at T and then turned to Lester. "I played him," she said. "I played him perfectly. We could have had sixty thousand dollars."

"Nah," Lester said, staring at T. He watched the bullet wound where blood welled up and spilled out. A rough black circle of blood spread across T's chest, saturating much of the shirt. "That's what you said, but that ain't it. You playing me, not him."

"That's not right."

"Yes, it is." He nudged T's foot. "How you doing there, bud?"

Weirdly, surreally, T heard himself answer, "I'm okay. You shot me."

"Sure did," Lester said. "Meant to put it through your heart. You should rightly be dead."

Jenny sat on the lip of the tub and rested her head on her fists. She looked like a little girl pouting. "If you were afraid Willie'd kill you anyway," she said, "we didn't have to go back. We could have taken the money and gone on ahead to Canada."

"Really?" Lester said. "Didn't you say no to that this afternoon? Didn't you say no way?"

"You didn't tell me what you were thinking," she said. "All you said was—"

"Shut up, Jenny." Lester raised the gun and pointed it at her temple.

Jenny backed away from the gun, into the wall. "Jesus Christ," she said. "You're planning on killing us both? Is that what you're thinking?"

"I knew this afternoon," Lester said. "When you were all we got to go back and pay off Willie. I knew right then, but I didn't want to believe it."

Jenny said, "You're wrong, honey."

Lester said, "I ain't wrong. And don't be calling me honey. It too late for that now."

Jenny clasped her hands over the back of her neck. "This is all just you're high," she said. "I can't believe you're doing this."

"It ain't all just I'm high." Lester climbed up on the john

and sat on the tank with his feet on the bowl. "You make me tired," he said to Jenny. "You know that? All these years. You make me tired."

"You're a sad case," Jenny said. "You're tragic." She looked back to T, her eyes moving from his face to the blood-soaked shirt and the bullet wound. "We had all that money," she said. "We had it in the palm of our hands."

Lester rested the gun on his knee. "Nah," he said. "That ain't it."

In the bathtub, with his feet sticking up ridiculously, T had the urge to pull himself into a more respectable position. He was acutely aware of his breathing, which went in and out, in and out, tossing his head back with each inhale and forward with each exhale—or at least it felt that way. Little movements seemed amplified. The burning under his collarbone had spread through the left half of his chest, spread and dulled so that now it was more like a throbbing heat. He lowered his eyes to look at the wound and saw that blood was still welling up out of it, and then he saw that it was spilling off him somewhere around his waist and collecting under him in the tub. He considered that the bloodstain on the back of his pants would be embarrassing once he stood up. He hated messes. He'd always hated messes. He was a neat man by instinct. He was a neat man by history. Even when he was a scruffy hippie, he was a *neat* scruffy hippie. Even when a child, when he was only a boy, he cleaned up after his parents. They were messy. They were bad. His father hadn't loved him. His father hadn't loved anyone. His mother left the dishes out overnight and hardly ever cleaned the house. They embarrassed him. The blood embarrassed him, the blood on the back of his pants. "Think someone might help me up?" he said. His voice was both harsh and whispery. He coughed.

"Where you want to go?" Lester said. He smiled. He had the look of a man amused by the innocent questions of a child.

"I'd like to get out of this bathtub," T said. He lifted his right arm and was pleased that he was able to do so without much pain. He knew for certain that lifting his left arm was going to be excruciating. He took a breath and the movement and the breath together seemed to clear his head a little, to wake him up some, as if he'd been sleeping.

"Look at you," Lester said. "You whiter than the bathtub. You scared?" he asked. "You that scared?"

"The guy's probably in shock," Jenny said. She turned to look at T and touched his calf gently. To Lester she said, "Do you want to sit here and watch him bleed to death?"

Lester tapped his knee with the gun. "I don't think so," he said. "That ain't the plan."

"There's a plan? You have a plan?"

"Uh-huh." He slid down from the john, grabbed the blue towel off the tank, and tossed it to Jenny. "Bandage that for him."

Jenny spread the towel open over her knees. "Want to get me something to cut this with," she said, "so I can make some strips?"

"Why would you want her to bandage me up?" T heard

himself say, loud, almost shouting. "Don't you mean to kill me?"

"We going fishing," Lester said. He disappeared a moment into the hallway and then returned with a penknife, which he tossed to Jenny. "You ever been night fishing, T?"

During the few seconds Lester was out of the bathroom, Jenny had turned to T and gestured with a vertical finger over her lips. Beyond telling him to keep quiet, he wasn't sure what the gesture meant, and he wanted to ask her. He thought there had been a look of resolve and collusion in her eyes, as if to suggest that she was with him, that he should trust her, that she would do what she could to get him out of this—but he thought that might have been wishful thinking on his part, and he wanted to hear her say it.

"Can you hear me all right?" Lester said. He leaned over the tub. "T?"

"I can hear you fine," T said.

"You soundin' a little better," Lester said, as if pleased.

"Help him out of there." Jenny had ripped the towel into several strips, which she laid out over the sink before she opened the medicine cabinet and rummaged through it, apparently looking for anything that might be useful.

Lester tucked the gun into his underwear and got into the tub to stand alongside T. He looked down at the blood that was now following a wide path to the drain. He positioned his feet on either side of the blood and started to crouch toward T, as if meaning to lift him up, but stopped suddenly and then flew into the tiled wall beneath the shower head as if a force had thrown him back. He gasped and stepped out of the tub, sliding against the wall, then backed out of the bathroom and into the hallway.

Jenny and T stared at Lester as he grasped the door frame to steady himself. "Whoa," he said. Then he laughed. "Fuckin' A."

Jenny said, "You're hallucinating now? What the hell did you take, Lester?"

Lester breathed deeply, laughing in between breaths, and then went back to the tub and lifted T out of it, one hand around the back of his neck and the other under his knees. "You just turned into my father," he said, putting T down on the john. "I mean, fuckin' unbelievable. You just, bang— There he was."

T said, "I'm not your father."

"Look at this," Lester said, holding his arms up and looking down at his chest. "You got blood all over me."

"Forgive me," T said. "Thoughtless of me."

Jenny stepped in front of T with the strips of towel flung over her shoulder, putting her body between him and Lester. She gave T a look which seemed to again ask him to be quiet. "So what are we doing?" she asked Lester, with her back to him. Gently, she grasped T's shirt by the collar and pulled it away from his chest.

Lester leaned over the sink to wash the blood off. "Just like I said." He found another towel and wiped himself off. "We making a mess of this place." He tossed the towel into the bathtub. "Ol' Chuck'll have a fit."

"What do you mean, just like you said?" Jenny cut away a piece of T's shirt and then folded a square of towel and pressed it hard against the bullet wound, sending a shock of electric pain through T from his toes to his forehead. He gritted his teeth and moaned. Jenny kissed him on the temple. "I'm sorry," she said coldly, and went about taping the towel over the wound with a roll of adhesive tape, which she must have found in the medicine cabinet.

Lester said, "I mean we goin' night fishing." He stood behind her and watched as she wrapped the remaining strips of towel around T's chest and shoulder and then taped them as best she could.

When Jenny was done with the bandaging, she washed her hands in the sink. "Lester," she said. "Please . . ."

Lester had taken a seat on the edge of the tub. "Please what?" he answered. To T, he said, "Can you stand up? Can you walk okay?"

"Please don't do this," Jenny said. She stood in front of him and placed the palm of her hand gently on his waist. "Can't you and I take a walk, try to talk this all over?"

"Help me with him," he said. He pushed her hand away and knelt on the right of T.

T said, "I don't need help." He leaned forward, shifting his weight onto his feet, and then lifted himself up slowly in spite of the green mosaic that blinded him as he rose and then dissipated only slightly as he tried to take a step and his knees started to buckle.

Lester held him up with an arm around the waist. T leaned against him reluctantly.

"Shit," Lester said. "Look at you. Walkin' with a bullet in you like the man!"

Lester laughed and then said something to Jenny about the guitar, about taking the guitar with them, and Jenny argued and he heard Lester say something back with a laugh, say *my stash*, but then T gave up on making out what they were saying because the loud buzz in his ears that had started softly grew deafening as they moved through the dark hall and toward the kitchen before it eased up some as they went out the back door. "What?" he said, but no one seemed to hear him, and he wasn't really sure he said it. After a few steps outside, down the hill, toward the river, the buzzing diminished and then it was completely gone, as were the green mosaics around his sight. He leaned against Lester as they walked along the grass. The moon was bright. It cast shadows through the trees. He concentrated on walking, putting one foot in front of the other. He thought Lester was probably taking him to the river to dump his body there. He imagined that Lester would shoot him again, probably in the head this time, or the heart, and so he thought he must be moving step by step closer to his death—and the only hope he had, far as he could think it through, was Jenny. How crazy was that? How strange? Out here under a pale bright moon on the Thousand Islands with a bare-chested murderer guiding him toward the last river, and the only hope of salvation this beautiful girl out of the dregs of the world, from the dregs, trying, T thought, probably her whole life to find her way out of the ugliness she was born into, and here she was his only hope when an hour ago she probably thought the opposite was true. "Jenny," he said. "Jenny?"

"She right here," Lester said, reassuring him.

"What is it, T?"

T heard her voice coming from someplace behind him. He didn't know why he had called out for her. He was sweating, and the walking was making him nauseous. "Can we stop a minute?" he said, and he tried to stop, but Lester tightened his grip around his waist and almost lifted him off the ground as he pushed him along.

"You be all right," Lester said. "You the man, T Walker."

T thought he might throw up. He concentrated on quieting the roiling in his stomach as Lester half carried him down the hill. A gust of wind picked up and then blew hard for a minute, sweeping over the ground, blowing leaves and small twigs against his calves and up his pant legs, and it felt good on his face, tousling his hair, and it helped him somehow to see more clearly the backs of the cabins passing to his right and the boulders and scattered rocks to his left along the narrow trail down the steep hill to the river. It was a beautiful windswept night, with the moon laying down a long, bright trail across the dark water so vividly T thought he might walk along it over the Saint Lawrence off into the horizon. For a moment he was filled up with the beauty of the place and the night, and then he remembered he was about to die. That was a hard thing to hold on to, that notion. He didn't really believe it. Why would he? It was out of his experience, as it always was with the living. He didn't believe it. He knew it was in the realm of possibility, he knew it was something that could happen, but he didn't think it actually would. Or at least part of him didn't. Part of him did, but part of him didn't. Lester might change his mind. Jenny might stop him. Lester might have a change of heart. The hand of God might descend and part the waters, and Lester might walk away into the depths. Only he didn't know that he actually believed in such a God, which he thought might be something he should be thinking about now.

"How are you doing?" Jenny said. She came up alongside him and touched his arm. She was carrying the guitar case like some kind of musician off to a midnight gig. To Lester she said, "He's sweating bad. Look at him."

"I'm all right," T said. "I'm a little dizzy."

"Lester," Jenny said. "Please, honey . . ."

Lester said, "Don't bother, Jenny. Ain't a thing bad 'bout to happen."

"For Christ's sake, Lester," she said. She lowered her voice. "He looks bad," she said. "What if he dies?"

Lester laughed. "What you think, Jenny? I shot him by accident?"

"I think you don't know what you're doing."

"I told you," Lester said. He stopped. They were at the

bottom of the hill, nearing the boulders where the boat was tied up. Water slapped against the shore and wind blew white wounds over the surface of the river. "I told you I'm perfectly clear," he said. "I'm high, but I ain't out of it. I'm inside it. Ain't that ever happen for you, Jenny? Where you know you seein' things the way they are and not the way you always dreamin' them? You know what I'm sayin'?"

"No," Jenny said. "I don't. You're not making sense."

"I'm making sense," he said. He shook T slightly. "How you holdin' up, bud?"

"Will you listen to me?" Jenny urged. A breeze roughed up her hair and she pushed it back off her face. "Think, Lester," she said. "When'd you ever kill anyone before? That's not you, Les. You're not a killer."

T said, "Are you going to dump me in the river, Les? Are you going to murder me?"

"Is that what you thinkin'?" Lester lifted T and continued along the trail to the boat. "Dying ain't nothin' to worry 'bout," he said. "There's no there there. There's no you here. That's all. But—" He stopped in front of the boat and looked over the scene. The stern tie had come loose, and the boat banged against the shore and rocked in the wind. There looked to be an inch of water in the bottom of the boat. "But we just going night fishin', T," he said. Then he added, "We got water in the fuckin' boat."

"Aren't you cold?" Jenny said to Lester. She laid the guitar down and sat on it.

"I'm not cold," Lester said.

T dropped suddenly toward Jenny, and he realized Lester was lowering him onto the guitar case. He sat down and leaned against her. He hadn't realized the degree to which he had been relying on Lester to hold him up until he had put him down.

Jenny put her arm around T. She looked up to Lester and laughed. "This is so absurd," she said. "Will you look at us? Will you look at this?"

T closed his eyes and took a brief vacation from the moment. Lester and Jenny continued to talk, but he didn't bother listening. He was tired, and things were so completely out of his control, it didn't seem important to pay attention. At least for a moment. He could take a moment's vacation. When Maura was a little girl she used to come into his bed in the morning to play with him. She'd wake up early, the way children do. Her mother was gone. Brooke had left them. Brooke left. He bought a house on Long Island. Huntington. Huntington, Long Island. In his house on Long Island, Maura woke early and climbed into bed. "Daddy," she said, "I'm a tiger, Daddy! Pick up your knees!" When T picked up his knees the quilt became a cave and tiny Maura, three-year-old Maura, climbed into the cave and became a tiger in the morning while T slept on and off, waking and sleeping, and Maura growled ferociously and leaped from the bed and came back dragging a stuffed animal in her mouth. Where was he then, sleeping and dreaming while Maura played? He was thinking about the day to come. Take Maura to Mom's, leave for work. Pick up salary checks. New hires. Chemicals, more stuff. Put the child away and go to work, Maura, Maura. Take her to Mom's, the little girl, the sweetheart. She was the cutest thing.

"T," Jenny said. "Come on. Get up."

T looked up into the moon behind Jenny's head. It was pale and white and huge. "Is that a full moon?" he asked.

Lester and Jenny both turned to look.

"See, now," Lester said. "Look at that. Full moon." He seemed to appreciate it. His eyes lingered on it a long moment.

"Looks like it could be a full moon," Jenny said. She knelt in front of T and wiped the sweat from his forehead with the hem of her dress. "T," she whispered, "you got to keep it together. He's hell-bent on going fishing."

Behind them, Lester had waded into the water. He went about untying the bow line and pulling the boat up onto the shore.

T said, "Please, Jenny." He gazed past her, to the water, where he could see Lester's back moving toward him, the tiger in the trees in the moonlight. Lester wrestled with the bow of the boat, pulling it up toward the rocks.

"I can't talk him out of it," Jenny said. "He's so fucking high he thinks he knows everything."

T said, "You've been dealing with stupid men your whole life, Jenny." He touched her leg and then leaned forward to rest his head on her knee. "I'm not stupid," he said. "He'll finish me off and dump my body in the river. You know that. You know that's what he's going to do."

Jenny said hurriedly, "I don't know what he's going to do.

Shit, *he* doesn't know what he's going to do. Look, what I know is something about being around guys who're wrecked. Anything can happen. Trust me on this." She glanced quickly behind her. Lester had worked the boat up halfway out of the water. He shook the river off his arms and legs like a wet dog. "There might still be ways out of this," she said. She kissed him, a quick peck on the forehead. "Come on." She offered him her hand.

When T tried to lift himself to his feet, the buzzing came back into his head, deafening him. He saw that Jenny was saying something; then Lester came up and said something too. He shook his head, trying to let them know he couldn't hear them. Lester leaned down and put his arm around T's waist, and the touch, which wasn't rough or hard, produced a jolt of unpleasantness in T that reminded him of touching an electrified fence, that dull, powerful heartbeat of something bad banging into him. "Wait, wait," he said, but Lester lifted him from the ground and carried him to the water the way a man would carry a child, one hand around his waist, the other under his legs. T went blind, the green mosaic occluding his sight. He couldn't see and he couldn't hear, but he knew that he was being carried, and then he was wet. He was sitting in water with his legs outstretched and his back against metal.

The water felt good. He was hot and water cooled. He didn't like water soaking his pants and shoes but otherwise it was good, cooling. After a minute the mosaic subsided and he saw that he was in the boat and that Lester and Jenny were on shore. He was in the bow of the boat. The current pulled the boat away from the shore, out to the wide river that was black under moonlight and white where the wind played on the surface. Lester and Jenny were talking on the shore while Lester held the stern line in his outstretched hand. T felt like a kid being pulled along in a wagon. The buzzing in his ears diminished and disappeared, as it had before, but the wind blew away whatever Jenny was saying to Lester and Lester to Jenny, back and forth, the wind blew it all away. He heard only water smacking the boat and rocks on shore, and wind over the water and through the trees.

In a moment of clarity, he thought that if he could stand and get to the stern, he might be able to yank the rope out of Lester's hand, and then he would float away. He could feel the current pull at the boat. The water was moving fast. He didn't think Lester would be able to swim out to him; the water moved too fast. The current was too fast. He could feel it pulling the boat out to the wide river, river like a rippling black sheet under the still white moon. He considered his situation. He might be able to do it. If he could yank the rope out of Lester's hand he'd float away and Lester couldn't catch him. Lester with his tigers: the one on his back, the one the girls had given him. Jenny and Lester on shore arguing in moonlight. Then they stopped arguing. Jenny threw her head back and stared up at the sky, sad, frustrated, a beautiful child made to stand in the corner. Across from her, Lester slumped solemn and unhappy. Together, they looked like a pair of ragged, rebellious children tired of being punished. The boy pulled a red wagon.

Winter is coming, window filled with frost. Words of a song came to T. *Don't say I never warned you when your train gets lost.* He was remembering pieces of lyrics from a song that seemed, far as he could see, apropos of absolutely nothing. "Hey," he called out, and Jenny and Lester turned to look at him. They seemed absorbed in their thoughts, his call a momentary distraction. They turned back to each other and resumed their argument.

T settled back in the bow. His pants were soaked. He wished he could go back in time and upload that single image he had so disastrously downloaded, send it back through the digital ether, return it to the hard drive from whence it sprang. He could draw a direct line from the moment he clicked on the make-believe button that said *download* to this moment when he was sitting in the bow of a boat in the dark bleeding to death. Though he didn't think he was bleeding anymore. He looked down at his chest. All he saw was a blue shirt cut away over his heart where a makeshift bandage made of towels was awkwardly taped to his chest and shoulder. He touched the bandage and looked at his fingers, and there was indeed blood on them. But he didn't feel like he was bleeding anymore. He felt numb over there. By his chest. By his heart. He felt numb. If he hadn't downloaded that picture, he wouldn't be here. That was certain. Imagine if he could have known at that moment what the consequences of such a simple, innocent act would be. It *was* innocent. He only wanted to look at a picture. How much more innocent can you get than wanting to look at a picture? It was a child-like act. It wasn't about lust; the lust was all in their corrupt minds. He found the picture interesting. Here was a girl feeding herself to a beast. He did look like a beast, that hairy back hunched over bulky and heavy, weighty like a beast. She was beautiful. She was perfect. And she was giving herself. In between was the woman, who was a mediator, a priest. She facilitated the offering. They wished it was rape. They wanted it to be rape. They denied what was in her eyes. They explained it away, making her pure victim, but she found her way into that trailer with that man and that woman the beast and the priestess and they seduced her or she let herself be seduced or whatever, what the hell did T know about it, what did any of them? It was a moment in time, a transaction. It was a picture. He would have liked to have figured it out. There was something in it that spoke to him about desire and beauty and innocence and experience. Maybe it was a horror. He had never denied that. Everyone wanted. The girl wanted. The man wanted. The woman. They wanted and were willing to transgress, all of them. He didn't know. T didn't. But there was such desire, such ecstasy of desire that the moment was incandescent. That he did know. That he could see. But for the most part he didn't know, he almost never did, and the ones who were sure, they had descended on him.

On shore, Lester took Jenny's chin in his hand, kissed her on the forehead, and then turned to the river and pulled the boat in. T had slumped down while waiting, and he pushed himself up with his good arm. He tried to sit up straight.

Lester pulled the stern of the boat up to the rocks before wading into the water and turning the boat around so that he was standing alongside T. "How you holding up?" he asked.

"Been better," T said.

"Bet you have," Lester answered. He seemed to be amused by T.

Jenny climbed out onto a flat rock, leaned over the boat, and put the guitar case down in the water at T's feet. "He looks like a man ready to go fishing," she said to Lester, and then she climbed into the boat and straddled the center thwart, situating herself so that she could see both Lester and T.

Lester pushed the boat off from the rocks and jumped into the stern. He primed the engine and started it on the third pull, and a moment later the boat was cutting through the water, driving away from the shore and out to the center of the river. Then suddenly he cursed and cut the motor. From the stern of the boat, near the engine, something rattled. It sounded like a chain slapping against the transom.

Jenny said, "What the hell is that?" The sound came again, several loud jolts of chain scraping on metal. The three of them were silent, listening.

"It's the fish," Lester said. He made a noise somewhere between a laugh and a shiver. "I forgot about them." He leaned over the stern and looked down into the water, and then the sound came again, the rattling of the fish pulling on the stringer.

Jenny said, "Let those things loose."

"Fuck no. We might need them for food."

"Need them for food?" Jenny said. Her tone of voice had gone beyond amazement into wonder. "We're going to need them for food? Did I hear you right?"

T said, "How many fish you got on, Les?"

"'Bout ten," Lester answered, still grinning at T.

"You're over the legal limit," T said. "If a ranger stops us," he added, "you could get in trouble."

A second passed, and then Jenny and Lester both laughed.

"You not in such bad shape," Lester said. "You still makin' jokes." He leaned over the transom, thrust his arm down into the water, and half lifted the stringer of fish out of the water before it jerked back violently out his hand. "Goddamn," he said.

T said, "What are you doing, Les?"

Lester unclipped the stringer, wrapped the top of the chain around his forearm, and grasped the bottom in both fists. "Want to show you the big one," he said. He crouched down and then yanked the stringer of fish out of the water and dropped it in the boat.

"Jesus God," Jenny said. She pulled her feet up onto the thwart.

T leaned forward to get a better look at the fish. They were all bass except for two pickerel and one big northern pike. The pike looked to be three feet long and weigh several pounds.

"Ain't this one a monster?" Lester said. He nudged the pike with his foot and it leaped up, splashing water and fish slime.

Jenny covered her face. "Please, Lester," she said, "get those things out of the boat."

"What do you think?" Lester asked T.

"Nice," T said. "Northern pike. Big one."

"Goddamn right," Lester said. He lifted the stringer up high to show off the full length of the big fish, and for the briefest of moments everything was still: there was only Lester with his youthful, muscular chest and his thick, long hair, proudly holding up a stringer of fish against the night sky. Then the big pike jerked violently and the chain ripped out of his hand. The pike bounced once in the bottom of the boat and went over the side. Lester lurched for the stringer and managed to get his hands around a bass, but it slipped instantly out of his grasp as the whole stringer disappeared into the river.

Lester sat back on the stern thwart and rested one arm on the engine. He watched the river where the stringer had cut through the surface and gone under and the water had closed up over it like a wound instantly healed. "Sum' bitch," he said softly. He stared at T a moment, his face solemn. "What do you think'll happen?" he asked. His voice was suddenly and strikingly gentle. "Will they all just pull in different directions until they kill each other or something?"

"About like that," T said. "Probably they'll die one at a time until the only one left alive can't drag all the dead weight, and then he'll die too."

"That's a pleasant thought," Jenny said.

Lester nodded. "Seem 'bout right." He pointed to the guitar case. "Open that thing up," he said to Jenny.

"What for?"

"For to get high," he said.

"Are you kidding?" She laughed and held the heels of her hands to her temples as if trying to keep her head from flying apart. "Lester," she said, "what are we doing? Please—"

"What?" he said, and gestured to the river around them. They were floating out toward the middle of the Saint Lawrence, toward the Canadian side, the American shore behind them a dark outline against the sky. "You got somethin' better to do?" he asked Jenny. "Bet you T wants to get high." He turned to T and raised his voice, as if talking to someone hard of hearing. "You want to get high, Tom?"

T didn't answer. He had fallen into a calm, distanced perspective on things. He felt free to observe what was going on and comment or not comment as he chose. The boat rocked slightly in the deeper water where it floated along, pulled by a swift current toward the shipping lanes. Jenny sat on the center thwart with her knees pulled up to her chin, her hair tossed about by breezes. Lester sat on the stern thwart and stared at him, waiting for an answer.

"T?" Lester repeated.

T chose not to answer.

"Fuck it, then." Lester leaned over the center thwart, alongside Jenny. "We getting' high," he said. He undid the snaps of the guitar case and flipped up the top. "What did Jenny tell you?" he asked T as he reached into the sound hole of the guitar and came up with a clear plastic zip-lock bag of multicolored pills. "She tell you poor innocent Jenny, fucked-up Lester ruinin' her life?"

"Why?" Jenny said. "Isn't that the truth?"

Lester found a pair of matching green gelatin capsules, popped them in his mouth, then reached over the side of the boat and scooped up a handful of water to wash them down. "These good," he said, pulling a black pill from the bag. He handed it to T. "Take this," he said. "You'll feel better."

T considered the pill. It looked like a rabbit pellet.

"Come on, take it," Lester urged. "I'm not fuckin' with you. You *needs* this."

T nodded, though he had no idea what he was nodding at or why. His concentration was focused on the guitar, on the resonant dark wood of the fingerboard, on the high polish of the body. It struck him as a lovingly and beautifully made thing, a work of art that like all works of art was something more than the sum of its parts. Resting in its case, cushioned and protected by a crimson, velvety padding, it called out to be touched.

"Open up," Lester said. When T didn't answer, Lester touched his chin with a fingertip, gently pulling his mouth open, and tossed the pill into the back of his throat.

T swallowed. "What's it going to do?" he asked.

"Make you feel better," Lester said.

Jenny said, "Why's life got to be like this, Lester?" She seemed completely serious. "A few hours ago, it was like a miracle. God drops all the money we need in our laps, plus some. Then you, you got to go and get spun. And now look at this." She gestured toward T. "Look at what you've done."

"Jenny," Lester said. He put the bag of pills back into the guitar and pulled out a fat joint. "You really think he give us that money? Really? You believe it?"

"Lester," Jenny said urgently, as if she'd just been offered an opening in an argument. "He's going to give us the money, Lester. We can still work this thing out."

"No," Lester said.

"Yes," Jenny said. "Me and him, we got something going between us, Les. We can still work this out."

Lester nodded and seemed to think about what Jenny had just said. "He going to give us sixty thousand dollars, Jenny?" He shook his head slowly, solemnly. "Think about it," he said. "You know it don't happen like that. He's givin' us sixty thousand dollars? I don't think so. Not us. Not likely."

"Lester, please," Jenny said. "You're not getting it. You're not seeing the whole picture. You're wrecked, honey. You're wrecked and you're missing the big picture."

"No I'm not," he said. He lit the joint with an old Zippo lighter, which he also pulled out of the body of the guitar. He inhaled and held the smoke in and stared Jenny down. "You ain't ever treatin' me with any respect, are you, Jenny?"

"Honey," she said, "I don't know what you're talking about."

"Even now, out here, like this." He gestured to the wide expanse of dark water around their small boat.

T leaned toward the guitar case and pushed the hard plastic top, which fell closed with a little whoosh of air, and then the guitar disappeared. "Like a mummy in a sarcophagus," he said. "The thing's airtight." He struggled to close the series of metal snaps that would lock the case.

"I got it," Jenny said. She and Lester were both watching T intently. Jenny closed the remaining snaps.

Lester said, "What you doing there, bud?"

"It's a beautiful guitar," T said, and then he leaned back, tired from the effort of closing the case. He laid his head down on the aluminum bow and looked straight up at the sky. He was amazed at the wide field of stars. He felt certain they hadn't been there a few moments ago. He would have seen them. They were so bright and big their light raged out of the black sky—and they went on forever, covering the earth like a dome. "Were there stars before?" he asked.

"Before what, T?" Jenny put her hand on his knee.

"Before," he said.

Jenny turned around on her seat so that she was facing Lester. She leaned close to him. "Listen to me," she said. "Start this thing up and take us back in."

"Yeah?" Lester said.

"Yes," Jenny answered. "We can take him to a hospital and tell them the truth. You got high. You shot him. It doesn't matter. You're going to have to change your name. You're going to have to do a whole new identity anyway."

"No, I'm not," Lester said.

"Yeah, you are!" Jenny shouted. "We get T to a hospital. You go on to Canada. When he's better, we'll pay off Willie. And then, Lester— Are you listening?"

"I'm listening," he said.

"Lester. You know I love you. I'm always going to love you. You're my brother. You're the brother I never had."

"Brother with benefits," he said.

"Stop," she said. She leaned in closer to him and put her hands on his knees. "I'll get you all the money you need. I won't leave you hanging. I'll get you the money you need to get started again. You can go back to school. You can study acting. You had talent, Les. You had real talent."

Lester nudged her aside so that he could see to the bow. "Hey, T?" he said. "When you all intimate with Jenny, back in the cabin? You know, when you and her *got something going* between you? She say I asked her to marry me? She tell you that? More than once, truth, over the years?"

"Lester," Jenny said. "Lester . . ." She pulled her legs up and buried her face in her knees.

T said to Lester, "I'd really like to figure this all out before you shoot me."

Lester said, "I already shot you, bud."

"Figure it out before you kill me," T corrected himself.

Lester said, "They ain't nothin' to figure out, T. Don't worry 'bout it."

Jenny reached toward Lester for the joint.

"There you go," he said, and handed it to her.

She took a long hit and looked up at the stars as she held in the smoke. A breeze rippled through the thin fabric of her sundress, and she folded her arms over her belly, holding the dress close.

T was thinking about Carolyn. He was considering the possibility that his life had gone fatally off course the moment she touched him in front of the fireplace that night when the snow was falling thick through a beam of light out her bay window in Syracuse. The thick flakes rocking slowly down. He lay on his back and watched snowflakes in the light while she undid his clothes, and he could still see the moment even now so many years later with Carolyn, what?, a skeleton inside a sealed box now, but then her fingers working on the buttons of his shirt amazed him. He had to look away, out the window to the snow. When he looked back she was pulling her sweater over her head. She undid her bra and he touched her breasts, but it wasn't the sex. She recited poetry: *things fall apart, the center will not hold*. She overwhelmed him. He became her companion, a kind of courtesan, there for the sex and to learn a thing or two at her feet, and that was what he was thinking about, that was what was going around and around in his mind: Did it start there? Because Alicia was right, no use now to deny it even though part of him still wanted to deny it. She was right. There was nobody there. There was nobody home, not really. He attached himself and tried to pretend he had a life. Brooke too. When he tried to think back to a point where what he wanted was what he wanted and not what Brooke offered or Alicia demanded, but his own, his own desires, when he tried to think back he had to go into his past before Carolyn. He wanted to be an artist. Before Carolyn he had a notion of himself as a poet. But Carolyn was a poet. She had published books of poetry. She had won prizes and awards for her poetry and of course what he wrote was worthless next to Carolyn and they both knew it and so he was quiet and he read her books and studied her poets and tried to learn from her while she recited from her vast store of poetry from Coleridge to Yeats to all the contemporaries and he learned to be quiet and listen though in the beginning it was with the idea that one day he would write great poems and he could still remember that, remember thinking that, and that was how far back he had to go to remember something he wanted that had nothing to do with anyone else. It preceded Brooke and Alicia and Carolyn and it had nothing to do with his parents, who were unread and uneducated. But after Carolyn, he never wrote another poem. He wasn't sure why. He started poems, he started many poems and stories over the years, but he never finished anything, and he was wondering now if she hadn't overwhelmed him, if his life might not have taken a different path had he not fallen in love with his professor. He fell in love with her. She cared nothing for him, not really; he understood that now. He was a boy. She played with him. He amused her. He was there for the sex and the amusement and she was there for her work, her writing, her scholarship. If he thought about it hard enough he could hate her. But he wasn't sure. It was only a theory. It could just as easily be an excuse. Carolyn could be someone convenient to blame. It was confusing. He was confused. He wished he could figure it all out.

"T," Lester said. "Tell me the truth." He sat with one arm up on the engine and he had begun tapping his feet again, heels moving rapidly in rhythm, his weight resting on his toes. "It don't make no difference now," he said. "Would you given us that money?"

T nodded. He would have given them the money. "Pretty sure I would have," he said. His head felt funny. He couldn't pinpoint the feeling. It was like an echo chamber stuffed with gauze. The whole left side of his chest throbbed and felt hot, but it wasn't hurting much. He wasn't hurting so much as he was weak and . . . dazed. He could think clearly for a minute or two and then the thoughts would shift and change. He knew he should be doing something about this situation, about Lester and the boat and Jenny and getting back to shore, talking Lester out of dumping him in the river, which he was sure was why they were out here—he was sure he was going to wind up floating along the bottom of the river—but he couldn't keep his thoughts together. They kept shifting. He would have given them the money. Why not? What did he care? "Money's not the issue," he said to Lester. "Money's not the problem."

"It's not?" Lester said. He laughed and hunched up his body so that he was sitting in the boat the way he had been sitting on the couch, leaning forward and tapping his feet.

Jenny said, "I told you he'd give us the money." She looked out across the river. She seemed pensive, as if she'd resigned herself to the situation for the moment at least and was taking some time to mull things over. She offered T a hit on the joint. T shook his head. "My uncle," she said. "The guitar uncle. He filled up a rowboat with rocks so that it could just barely still float. Then he tied himself to the seat—"

"Why you tellin' him that story?" Lester interrupted.

"What?" Jenny said. "Why not? Why shouldn't I?"

"Just shut the fuck up 'bout that. I don't want you tellin' him that story."

Jenny said, "You're so out of it, Lester." She nodded her head toward the gun stuck in his underwear. "Aren't you afraid you're going to blow your balls off?"

"Hey, T?" Lester said. "You know why you're out here?"

T met Lester's eyes for a moment and looked at him as if he might be able to understand something more about him by observing the weathered features of his face, the way his skin looked seared by time—but in the end Lester's face told him very little. It was a youthful face, though worn and battered. A few years ago he had seen an exhibit of Richard Avedon's photographs. He had wandered before the trademark black-and-white portraits of the rich and poor, the good and bad, famous and unknown, and he had come away with the same feeling, that in the end the body tells you next to nothing. For all its uniqueness, it reveals nothing essential at all. He forgot what Lester had asked. He laid his head down on the bow and returned his gaze to the stars.

Lester turned his attention back to Jenny. "I always liked Ronnie," he said.

Jenny said, "He was a sweet man."

"T!" Lester yelled.

T pulled himself back into the boat. He had been sailing up toward the stars, leaving the little boat with Jenny and Lester under him on the black river while his body floated up like one of the childhood images from church on Sundays of Christ ascending to the heavens. He half expected Mary to appear alongside him and the cherubim to join them blowing trumpets. Yet he hadn't missed any of Lester and Jenny's conversation. "Must have been a mini hallucination," he said.

"I'm sure," Lester said. "Whatever."

"I think so," T said.

Lester said, "You know who I am?"

T said, "I know who you are. I'm okay. I think I might have half fallen asleep."

"That's good," Lester said. "You know why you're out here, T?"

T nodded. "Because I downloaded the wrong picture."

Lester leaned back and laughed.

"Jesus," Jenny said. "You're both out of it."

Lester opened the guitar case, found the bag of pills, and pulled out two more black ones. He handed them to T. "Take these," he said. "You need these, buddy. One ain't doing the trick."

Jenny said, "What are you giving him?"

"What the fuck do I know?" Lester said. "All I know is, three of these things he should be feelin' no pain."

T took the pills. When he tried to swallow them, he gagged and Jenny scooped up a handful of river water and spilled it gently into his mouth. The water was soothing and the pills went down. "Thank you," he said, and he gestured toward the open guitar case. "Snap that closed," he said. "Will you, please?"

Jenny closed the guitar case and snapped it shut. She said, "How come you're so worried about this guitar, T?"

T shrugged. He didn't know why. It was beautiful. It was something beautiful in the boat with them.

Lester said, "Ronnie bought that guitar in New York. She tell you that?"

T shook his head.

"Bought it from a guy said he was a classical musician."

Jenny said, "Ronnie tell you that story?"

"Claimed to pay a thousand dollars for it. This back 1960."

"He did," Jenny said. "Babs said he did. She said he came back from New York broke and with the guitar."

"Guy was playin' in the subway. He couldn't believe how good."

"He was always the sweet one," Jenny said. "He was the one would take care of us."

"You remember that?" Lester said. "You remember how he'd come around and get me sometimes?"

Jenny closed her eyes and sighed as if despairing.

"He'd come around and get me when Daddy on a drunk. He'd take me out campin' by the lake. Sometimes I live in that trailer out there with him a week 'fore I could go home."

Jenny said, "Jesus, Lester. You're telling me this like I wasn't out there with you half the time."

T imagined the two of them as a pair of ragged kids playing together by the water, climbing trees in their worn-out sneakers and dirty jeans.

Lester was quiet a while, looking off at nothing. Then he turned to Jenny again, his eyes dark and narrowed to a glare. "Why you doin' me like this?" he said. "Jenny? Why'd you do me this way?"

"Lester, honey," she said, "I don't know what you're talking about."

"Yeah, you do," he said. "You got no respect for me. You show me no respect. You think I'm stupid."

"No, I don't," she said. "I don't think anything like that."

"You know how I know when you lyin', Jenny?"

"No, Lester," she said, indulging him. "How do you know when I'm lying?"

"When I see your lips movin'."

"You're just being mean," she said. "You don't believe that."

"Fuck I don't," he said. "Whether T here gives us the money or not won't make no difference for me 'n' you know it. Willie'll kill me anyway, and you think I'm too stupid. You walk me right back there like I mean nothin', like I never meant nothin' to you."

"That's not true."

"Fuck it ain't." He raised his voice to T. "I'm askin' you again, T? You know why you out here?"

T's head felt a little clearer, some of the stuffiness gone and the sense of being dazed diminishing. "Not really, I guess," he answered. "I guess I don't really know why I'm out here."

"You out here because of Chucky," he said, looking at

Jenny. "The dude whose cabin this is," he went on, turning to T. "He's why you out here."

Jenny said, "What's Chuck got to do with it? What's going on in your drugged-up head, Lester?"

"Chuck's got to do with it is he put you up to it. You think I didn't know all along, Jenny? You think I'm that dumb?"

"Is that what you think happened? Oh, Christ, Lester— Is that what you think happened?"

"Is that what I think?" Lester echoed Jenny. *"Them Mexicans, Les. They won't give you no trouble."*

"Oh, for God's sake, Lester. How could I have known what they'd do?"

"Shit." Lester spit over the side of the boat, as if he were angry at the river. He leaned back on the engine and looked past Jenny to T. "Me robbin' Short Willie," he said. "I'm not that crazy. I did it 'cause I knew her uncle Chuck behind it, and I figured he might could pull it off. Chuck the biggest slime bag around. Sum' bitch the biggest crook in Tennessee."

"So what?" Jenny said. She crossed her arms over her chest. "So what if you're right? How's that change anything?"

"You set me up's how it change things."

"I didn't."

"Yeah, you did. And you doin' it again, go back there and get killed and you run back here to him."

"For Christ's sake, Lester." Jenny looked over the side of the boat as if she were considering jumping out. "I can't talk sense to you when you're like this. What in hell would there be in it for me if I set you up? You don't get the money, I don't get the money. What in hell reason would I have for setting you up? Chuck said we could make five, six thousand apiece. You're right about that, okay? He did. I didn't tell you that I knew about the Mexicans from Chuck because he told me not to tell you. He said what you didn't know couldn't come back to bite you, and I took him at his word."

"That always a mistake," Lester said.

"Why would I set you up, Les? Will you ask yourself that? What possible reason could I have?"

"Not just you settin' me up," Lester said. "Chuck doin' it through you and you playin' along."

"I don't know what you're talking about, Les."

"Let me ask you this," he said. He paused a second and stared at her. It was as if they had forgotten T was in the boat. Their eyes were fixed on each other. "Let me ask you this," he repeated. "It occurred to you he might could be setting you up too? He might could plan this whole thing to happen just the way it happen? He figure I come runnin' to you. He figure Willie find out me and you in it together."

"Why?" She threw up her hands. "Why, Les?"

T picked up the guitar case and held it to his chest. He wrapped his arms around the neck and supported himself with it. "Lester," he said, "maybe I can help."

Lester's eyes were sad. He looked incredibly tired. "They ain't no help anymore, T. Kinda sorry you out here now. I was startin' to like you."

"I was thinking, money," T said. "I could—"

"You not all that bad."

"Answer me," Jenny said. "Why would Chuck do something like that to me?"

"That a good question, Jenny. Why would Uncle Chuck do you that way?"

"I don't know," she said. "Why would he? You know something I don't?"

"Let me ask you this, Jenny. D'you ever wonder why Johnny kept them pictures of you? Of his own daughter?"

"No," she said. "I didn't. He was a man. Men are like that."

Lester's face twisted up sour. "He was your father."

"No, he wasn't."

"That don't matter," Lester said. "He was your father, and I don't think he had them to look, like everyone said."

"You don't? You got a different theory?"

"Chuck stopped hangin' around with you, didn't he? I'm told Chuck stopped turning up with you places like he used to."

"What are you trying to say, Les? Spit it out."

"I don't think Johnny was lookin' at those pictures. He never struck me a sick sum' bitch like his brother."

"So what do you think, then? Let's hear it."

Lester looked away from Jenny, first at T and then out to the water and up to the stars and then back to T. He seemed to be recalling where they were, out on the Saint Lawrence, a mild October night under a bright field of stars in a small boat with a man he'd shot. "I think Johnny must've stole them pictures away from Chuck. I think he kept those pictures to blackmail him," he said softly, almost reluctantly. "To make him stay 'way from you," he added. "To make him leave you 'lone."

It took Jenny a minute to respond, and in the silence a breeze rippled over the water and rushed through the boat, pushing her hair off her face and wrapping her dress tight to her body. She nodded to Lester, as if to say he was right. "And to extort money from him," she added. "So he could drink it up and spend it on whores, like he always did."

"Jenny," Lester said, his voice dropping into a deeper register, coming from someplace low in his body. "He's your uncle, Jenny. The bastard your uncle."

"No, he's not," she said. "You know that."

"But you didn't," he said. "You didn't know that until the trial. And it don't matter anyway."

"Yes, it does," she said. "And I did know. I've known since I was thirteen that Johnny wasn't my father and Chuck wasn't my uncle. Chuck told me, first time, when I was thirteen."

Lester stared at her in silence a long moment. "Since you were thirteen," he said. "That how long it been going on?"

"Since I was thirteen."

Lester looked deeply sad. He shook his head. "Hey, T?" he said, and he pointed out over the gunwale. "That the ocean out that way?"

T looked out where he was pointing, down the center of the wide channel, east toward the ocean. He nodded.

Lester squeezed the bulb on the gas-tank line a few times and then positioned himself to pull back on the engine cord.

"What are you doing?" Jenny asked.

"What's it look like?" He pulled the cord and the engine started easily.

"So what did any of that have to do with why Chuck might set us up?" The boat started moving, and Jenny pushed her hair off her forehead and held it out of her face with one hand pressed flat over the top of her head. "You think he knew they'd rob you, the Mexicans?" she said. "You think he knew Willie'd come after both of us? That's what you're saying?"

T wanted to interrupt them a moment, just long enough to tell Jenny how beautiful she looked that way, with her hair pushed back, in the moonlight, the wind riffling her dress.

Lester said, "I'm nothin' but shit to you." He leaned a little closer to Jenny, as if to be sure she'd hear him over the growl of the engine. "Chuck's disrespected and fucked with you your whole life," he said, "and you in love with that ugly son of a bitch."

Jenny said, "You got a simple mind, Lester. You think everything's simple."

"Maybe," he said, "but I'm seeing clear now. I'm inside it now," he said. "Now it all perfectly clear."

"You're spun, Les. That's the only thing perfectly clear."

Lester's face seemed to sink into itself. He looked suddenly old and worn as he leaned still closer to Jenny. "He tired of you," he said. "You weren't so blind about him, you'd see it too. You come back to town, go back to school. You expectin' that job he been promising you since forever..." He stopped and wiped away sweat from his upper lip. "He tired of you, Jenny. He got rid of you. That's all. He tired of you and he got rid of you and it don't mean nothin' someone like him someone like me gets killed. And don't hurt either he'll make a few dollars in the deal."

"That's crazy," Jenny said. "That's just crazy."

"No, it's not," he said. "Once you get clear about things, it obvious really." He sat back on the transom with the engine rudder in his left hand and steered the boat out toward the ocean. "It all perfectly clear to me now," he said. "I ain't shit to you, I ain't never been. I see that now. It clear now. You twisted around that evil fuck and he played you and I got played with you. That's all. That's all this is."

"You're wrong," she said. "Chuck wouldn't do that to me." She looked out over the bow. "What are you doing, Les?" she asked. "Where are we going?"

Lester said, "You so sad, Jenny." While she was still looking away from him, out to the ocean, he put the gun to her forehead almost gently and held it with both hands as he fired. Her body flew over the side and into the river and he turned to watch as it fell behind them and only when it had disappeared under the water did he look back to T.

At the sight of Lester pulling out the gun, T had used the guitar as a crutch and partially lifted himself to his feet. Then he fell back at the gunshot, so that he was sitting on the bow with his arms wrapped tightly around the neck of the guitar case.

Lester said, "It a sordid life," and raised the gun listlessly.

T jumped back and then fell off the boat and into the water with the guitar case. He watched the engine roar past as he followed the path of the boat, expecting it to turn around and come back for him. Instead, the engine roared louder and the bow lifted higher and then there was another flash and the pop of the gun firing and Lester flying backward over the transom and disappearing instantly in the boat's wake.

Alongside T, the guitar case floated top up, the snaps six inches above water. T grasped it under his good arm and found that he could lean most of his weight on it without submerging the snaps. He laid his head down on the hard plastic and watched the little sliver of aluminum boat until it finally disappeared into the darkness, leaving him alone with the silence and the water and the raging stars.

. 4 .

When he leaned a little to the right, sliding his cheek along the wet plastic of the guitar case, he could see the hole in his chest. Hours ago the last scrap of bandage had floated away, revealing raw, puckered skin around a blood-black, dime-sized puncture in the alarming vicinity of his heart. He clutched the guitar case, careful to keep the snaps above water. All night it had carried him through the darkness, holding to the surface of the Saint Lawrence so resolutely he thought the thing could be marketed as a life preserver—as long as he kept the water out of it, kept the sea from seeping into it. He concentrated on that, on keeping the guitar case flat as he floated through the last minutes of night, his eyes on the horizon, waiting for the sun to emerge out of the river. It was easier now to keep the guitar case level, now that morning was near and the sea was so still it reflected the stars and the moon, now that the wind had died down to nothing. Earlier, in the deep hours of night, he had struggled to keep hold, his arm wrapped tightly around the solid plastic case as wind slicked his hair against his head and whipped the surface of the water into froth. He had fought all night to hold on, aided by Lester's black pills, which were wearing off now. He could feel them wearing off, and as their effects faded, so did his strength. As first light neared, he clung to the guitar case with the mild hope of being seen. He reminded himself that this was the Saint Lawrence Seaway and many ships traveled these lanes, and if he could just hold on till it was fully light, if he could keep his one good arm wrapped tightly around the guitar case and keep the thing flat so the water wouldn't get in, if he could keep it from tilting and hold on a little longer it would be light soon, and he was floating in the shipping lanes and he might be seen. He told himself that he had held on already through the night and the sky was growing lighter as the stars faded, though the moon was still bright. But it was getting harder. His body wanted to loosen its grip and his mind had to have a talk with it. He had to explain. Morning was coming. It would be light. A ship might see him.

Night had seemed endless. Lester was right, though: through the long hours, thanks to the black pills, he had felt no pain. But neither was his mind right. On and off he had slipped into a kind of waking dream: the hard black guitar case once became a downy white pillow and his head sank into it as it shaped itself to the contours of his face. For a brief moment, the guitar turned into a boat pulling him to shore. At another point, the neck of the guitar was a corridor he swam into out of rough water, like swimming onto a beach, only when he lifted himself up out of the waves he was at the head of a long hallway, bathed in reddish light. He shook the sea from his body and found himself dry and dressed comfortably in jeans and T-shirt. Barefoot, he walked in the red light and he knew the corridor was actually the neck of the guitar and he was walking toward a place he all along had been meant to find, a place that was like a mountain in sunlight or a meadow thick with wildflowers, a place that sang to him, a place where he was meant to look, to smell, to hear, to touch, and he walked toward it along the red corridor only to find himself suddenly again out on the black water with a stinging mist blowing into his eyes, struggling to keep from drowning, to keep from joining Lester and Jenny at the bottom of the river.

He imagined them, Lester and Jenny, floating alongside each other, their bodies bouncing lazily off rocks, bumping along the bottom pushed by currents, their long hair trailing behind them, rippling luxuriously strand by strand, rising and falling in the deep water's swells. He saw Jenny's beautiful hair. He saw her watery eyes open, still looking east over the river, wondering where Lester was taking her. She had no idea what was coming. None at all. She was only looking out over the river and wondering where they were going. In the riled water, holding on for his life, T mumbled, "What chance did she ever have?" and he was thinking not only of that final moment on the boat but of her life. He thought, *She was seduced and betrayed while she was still a child,* and a moment later he found himself recalling the pornographic image he had downloaded, the one that had started all his trouble, and then he was there, inside that trailer, just outside the frame of the image, as if in a kind of cosmic dark that surrounded the real world or in a shadowy darkness beyond the lighted image.

The woman and the girl were stretched out on the sofa, and the woman stroked the girl's hair and cooed sweet sounds into her ear. T in the darkness was amazed that he could hear those sounds, and he realized that being able to hear was the striking difference between being there and just seeing the picture. There, in the shadows, in the surrounding dark, he heard the woman whispering promises into the child's ear, and there, so close, he saw clearly that the girl in her arms was a beautiful child, and he knew somehow that she was more beautiful in that moment than she would be ever again. It was as if it were the child's last moment and he knew it, and then a man who had been standing beside him in the darkness stepped into the light and T knew immediately at the sight of that bulky, hirsute body what was about to happen. He watched with his heart racing as the man approached the child and the child turned her cheek into the woman's breast and opened her mouth. He could see that the child was full of the woman's words and she wanted what was about to happen, and then he was there, at the exact erotic moment arrested in the photographic image, only now, when the man entered her and T heard the sound that issued from the girl's lips, instead of the sensual moan he had imagined, a groan of pain rose up out of the belly of the child, a sound agonized and terrible. T saw her locked in the woman's arms, and then he was in the next moment, the moment after the moment in the image, and he saw the child crying for all that was lost and all that would follow, and, in the next moment, she looked at him. She found T in the shadows, her eyes met his eyes, and T was ashamed. He closed his eyes to hide from her gaze. When he opened them again, he was back on the Saint Lawrence and the river around him for as far as he could see was littered with the bodies of young women, multitudes of bodies floating under the eye of the moon. For several long moments he could not shake it off, that vision of countless young women, raped, beaten, murdered, bruised, in shackles, in chains, all of them floating out to sea, all of them beautiful.

In time the river returned to black waves and white froth, and it held him for hours more as his thoughts settled and calmed, though they also grew fuzzier, less distinct, the clarity of that terrible image lost as he recalled a long sequence of memories involving his own children, the most vivid a memory of the red maple in their front yard shedding leaves in an autumn wind, in a leaf storm, the red and yellow leaves falling thick as snowflakes, and the kids, Evan and Maura, running wildly through the falling leaves with their arms outstretched, yelling in the big wind, their open mouths full of joyful shouts. After a time, even those memories disappeared and he was left with a growing pain in his chest and arm, a pain that threatened to overwhelm him, and he slid his head along the slick black plastic to look at the hole in his chest. The sky overhead was beginning to lighten, the stars and moon beginning to fade, and out of somewhere something howled, a piercing growl, and he looked down into the bright yellow ball of the sun high on the horizon. Below him, he could feel Lester and Jenny swimming in the depths, as if trailing beneath him, and he tried to tell Lester, no, no, it's not, the world is not what he, what Lester, said, but then T let that go, that desire to tell, and he held Maura's hand and Evan's hand and he focused entirely on the wavering yellow ball of the sun flickering over the green surface of the water, and then there were men in bright orange jackets trying to speak to him, only they spoke in tongues, they babbled, and then they were behind and alongside him as the guitar was pulled away and his body floated, held in Carolyn's loving arms, and various memories fluttered through his mind like Carolyn's snowflakes rocking lazily down as he was lifted into the hum and vibration of movement, into the skimming over water, the jostle and lurch, until a black wall of steel bore down on him and he struggled to find Carolyn in the stern at the engine and saw instead a bright orange jacket wrapped around a bearded man. T said, "Carolyn's dead," and the orange jacket beside him said *okay, okay* and nodded as he wrapped a blanket around him and then there was a great whirring sound as they rose out of the water, pulled up along a black wall into the heavens.

Epilogue

During the invasion of Iraq, T fell in with a group of fellow Americans in Crete. Nights they huddled together to watch the massive bombing of Baghdad and days they looked over their shoulders, concerned for their own safety. It was a time of quick friendships and T found himself in the regular company of an American writer and his physician wife, a pair of decent, generous people around whom a kind of old-fashioned salon revolved. They opened their home to artist friends from all over the world, most of whom only visited for a week or two, though one woman, an artist in her late forties, had been staying with them when T arrived in January and had no immediate plans to leave. Between the writer and his wife and their friends, there were always a half-dozen or so people with whom he might enjoy a social evening, or a late dinner at the Argentina, or a day of hiking and swimming.

Typically, though, he spent his days exploring the beaches on the coast or the mountains of the interior. It was his habit to get up before dawn and sit out on his deck with a cup of Turkish coffee, where he watched the sun come up over the Aegean, the bright circle of light arising as if out of the sea itself. After breakfast he'd gather up his maps and guidebooks, pick an interesting spot somewhere on the island, drive to it, and spend the day exploring and taking pictures. He shot a roll or two most days, then on Saturdays went into Hania, where he had contact sheets made. In the four months he'd been taking pictures, he'd managed a dozen shots he liked enough to have enlarged and framed. Several of them he'd already given away, to the writer and the doctor and their friends; the others were in his study; one, his favorite, a shot of the late-afternoon sun exploding into an offshore cave, he had hung in his living room. He intended, sooner rather than later, to build a dark-room behind the kitchen.

His brief, violent weekend with Jenny and Lester had already settled into a dreamy memory. Sometimes it seemed impossible that he had picked up a pair of young hitchhikers and almost paid for that bit of recklessness with his life. After his hallucinatory night on the Saint Lawrence, he had spent close to a month in the hospital recovering from complications caused by the gunshot wound, which by itself had done limited serious damage, but the bullet had lodged close to his heart, and after much debate the doctors had gone in and removed it. During his hospital stay, Alicia had come to visit him, as had Maura and Evan. Alicia had entered the room guardedly, clearly not knowing what to expect, given he had pretty much thrown her out of his house the last time they'd met. When he apologized to her for all that had gone wrong between them, when he told her he wanted to let it go and move on, she only nodded at first, and then she touched his leg—she was sitting alongside his bed—and laid her head down on the mattress, her forehead against his thigh. She looked away from him as he stroked her hair.

Soon after Alicia's visit, Maura came; and then a week later Evan walked through the door. He sat in a chair near the foot of the bed. His first words were, "Mom said I should come to see you," which he issued as if a challenge, as if to reassert his anger. T told him how glad he was to see him, how much it meant to him that he had made the trip. Evan nodded. When the silence thickened, T told him about his night on the water, as he had told Alicia and Maura before him. He told him about the hallucinations, the travels he had taken inside the body of the guitar—and he told him how, on the edge of losing consciousness, his mind had taken comfort in memories that were so intense they felt real, as if he were back again living through them—and he told him that one of the last things he remembered was Maura and Evan as children shouting and running wildly through a big wind in autumn, the air around them thick with a blaze of brightly colored leaves. Evan said yes, he remembered that too. Then he got up and touched T's shoulder and said he was sorry but he had to leave.

Within a month of being released from the hospital, T had sold his house in Salem, given away or sold most of his possessions, and moved to Crete, where already he felt more at home than he ever had in Virginia. He found his villa comforting, with its view of the Aegean, its thick stone walls and oak bookcases, and its growing collection of art he was acquiring from visiting painters, as well as from a local gallery in Hania, where he had developed a friendly relationship with the owner, a thin Greek woman in her fifties with a caustic sense of humor and a genial smile. Time seemed to move more slowly in Crete, and in a good way, not the way it had slowed down in Salem, thickening in the air, suffocating him, but in a comfortable way, in a slower pace, in an atmosphere that allowed him to breathe easily as he moved among the island's mythic places, looking, and taking pictures.

He thought a lot about Carolyn. He was reading her books of poetry again, working his way deep into them. He was coming to see her as a kind of storm force of intellect and talent that had swept over him as a young man. It didn't seem necessary anymore to keep his relationship to her a secret. He had even written about her to Maura and Evan, though he was writing to them about everything in his life. He had taken to writing them twice a week, long letters in which he talked about his past and tried hard to explain himself, and to convince them that they were both immensely important to him. Maura had begun writing back. Evan had called a few times. He planned to keep writing to both his children, the letters having become a twice-a-week ritual. He kept all of the letters in a computer file, and nights he'd sit in front of the glowing monitor and read through them.

He didn't think about Jenny and Lester much anymore. He remembered them as tragic figures whose lives had intersected with his for a fiery instant. When he thought back to that weekend, he wound up thinking about his time on the water. He had been out of his mind for most of that night, but not so out of his mind he hadn't known to cling to the guitar. He had been picked up by an Argentinean freighter, though he remembered very little beyond the vivid images of rising up into the early morning sky as their dinghy was hauled by winch up the side of the ship. Now the restaurant where he had dinner so many nights, a Greek restaurant on a Greek island, was called the Argentina. Did that mean something? Was there a message there somewhere? If there was, he didn't get it. He was a rube scratching his head before the work of a masterful magician. All he knew was that he didn't know much of anything beyond that he wanted to live. You don't cling all night to a guitar case while floating in the Saint Lawrence with a bullet lodged near your heart unless you want very much to live. He did. He would. Nights in his villa, when he was finished reading whatever book he was reading, or tinkering with the red guitar, or rereading his own letters, he'd turn off the lights and get into bed and stare out his open window at the sea. Sometimes in the moments right before sleep, those moments that are like floating on water, the shame he felt that night on the Saint Lawrence, when that child's eyes searched out his eyes and found him watching in the dark, that shame returned so vividly that he had to get out of bed and turn on the lights, because he knew if he closed his eyes he'd see the nightmarish hallucination of an ocean littered with the bodies of murdered women. Those nights he'd get dressed and walk along a dirt-and-cobblestone road that wound its way along the Aegean and into the village, where he'd usually find someone still talking over wine or raki at the Argentina, and he'd join them, taking part in the conversation, which somehow, always, for reasons he didn't understand, helped him reclaim a sense of his own decency, just sitting at a table over food and drink and talking about each other and the world. Sometimes he'd spend half the night there, among Greeks who it seemed could talk forever. Often he was the first to leave, to get up amid the chatter and laughter, to finish off his drink and start back for his cottage, looking forward to the quiet walk along a seaside road.